NOTHING BUT TROUBLE

Nothing But Trouble

Bob Thurber

photography by Vincent Louis Carrella

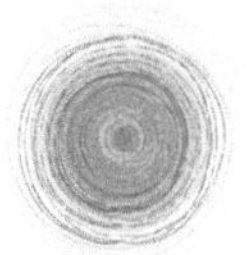

Shanti Arts Publishing

Brunswick, Maine

Nothing But Trouble

Published by Shanti Arts Publishing.
Cover and interior design by Shanti Arts Designs.

Shanti Arts LLC
193 Hillside Road, Brunswick, Maine 04011
shantiarts.com

Printed in the United States of America

First edition
10 9 8 7 6 5 4 3 2 1

Publisher's Cataloging-In-Publication Data
(Prepared by The Donohue Group, Inc.)

Thurber, Bob.
Nothing but trouble / Bob Thurber ; photography by Vincent Louis Carrella. -- First edition.

pages : illustrations ; cm

ISBN: 978-0-9885897-6-6 ebook ISBN: 978-0-9885897-7-3

1. Short stories, American. 2. Domestic fiction. I. Carrella, Vincent Louis. II. Title.

PS3620.H86 N68 2014
813/.6 2014935573

Dedication

For Colleen, who has always been so wonderfully no trouble at all.

Acknowledgments

Unnecessary Impressions - Second Place by Amy Hempel in *Lumina*'s (Sarah Lawrence College's Literary Magazine) National Flash Fiction contest. **My Daily Bread** - Second Prize in Fiction, *FlashQuake,* Fall 2001. **Not The Real Jesus Christ** - *Smokelong Quarterly,* December 2004; *Smokelong Anthology,* August 2005; Nominated for the 2005 Million Writers Award. **Dry Socket** - *Sterling Magazine,* April 2013. **The Baby's Name** - *Rumble Magazine,* November 2009. **Lost and Found** - Honorable Mention in the *Geist* Literal Literary Postcard Story Contest, 2007. **The Stray** - Finalist for the Marjory Bartlett Sanger Award, unpublished. **Wooden Matches** - First Prize, *Newport Review*'s 2007 Flash Fiction contest. **Cryptogram** - *Iowa Review Web,* September 2003. **Crackers** - *The Café Irreal* #40. **Mister Fumble Bumble** - *The Café Irreal* #40. **Mismatch** - "9 Fictions," *Oasis Journal,* July 2002. **Door Prize** - Second Prize, Missouri Writer's Guild Flash Fiction Contest, unpublished. **Old Sharp Photo** - *The Café Irreal* # 45. **A Woman on the Bus** - *The Café Irreal* #38. **Entry Level** - First Place, *Word Riot*'s Flash Fiction Contest, February 2003. **A Proper Investigation** - First Prize in Fiction, *FlashQuake,* Spring 2002. **Loot** - Finalist for World's Best Short-Short-Story Contest, *The Southeast Review,* April 2005. **Seaside Hitchhiker** - The 2005 Marjory Bartlett Sanger Award from The New England Writer's Association; published in three anthologies. **The Cat Who Waved** - *The Café Irreal,* February 2001. **Tarzan's Dream** - *Diagram* 2008. **Six Crows** - *In Which,* Fall 2001. **Simple Decoration** - Firebox Fiction Award, *Night Train Magazine,* April 2003, performed on National Public Radio (KRCB) as part of a holiday special, December 2004. **You Don't Belong Here** - *The Café Irreal* #34. **The Manuscript** - Firebox Fiction Award, *Night Train Magazine,* 2003; Finalist for the Marjory Bartlett Sanger Award, July 2004; Student Choice Award, Whidbey Writers' Workshop, July 2009. **In The "Nick Of Time" Redux** - *Sublit,* December 2007. ■

Unless you're filthy rich, life is nothing but trouble,
so you damn well better get used to it.

~ standard advice from Frieda, mother of the author

Contents

(continued)

Images

(continued)

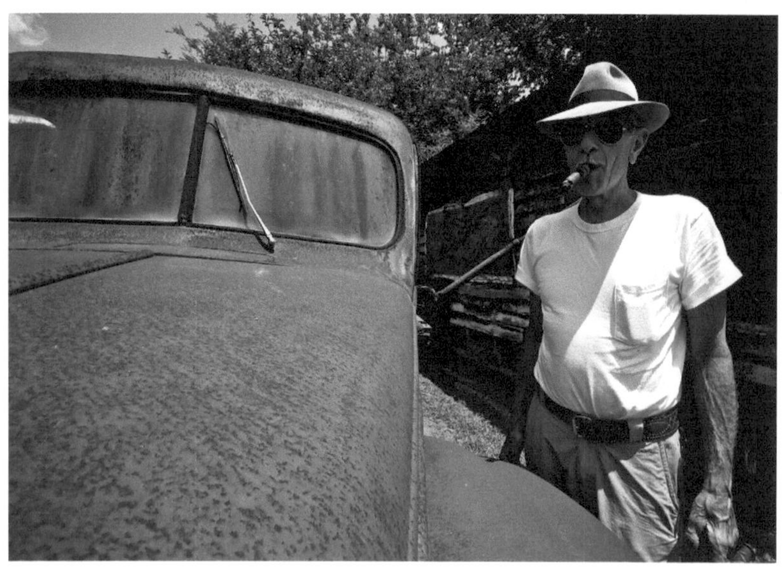

Fathers and Fools

Unnecessary Impressions

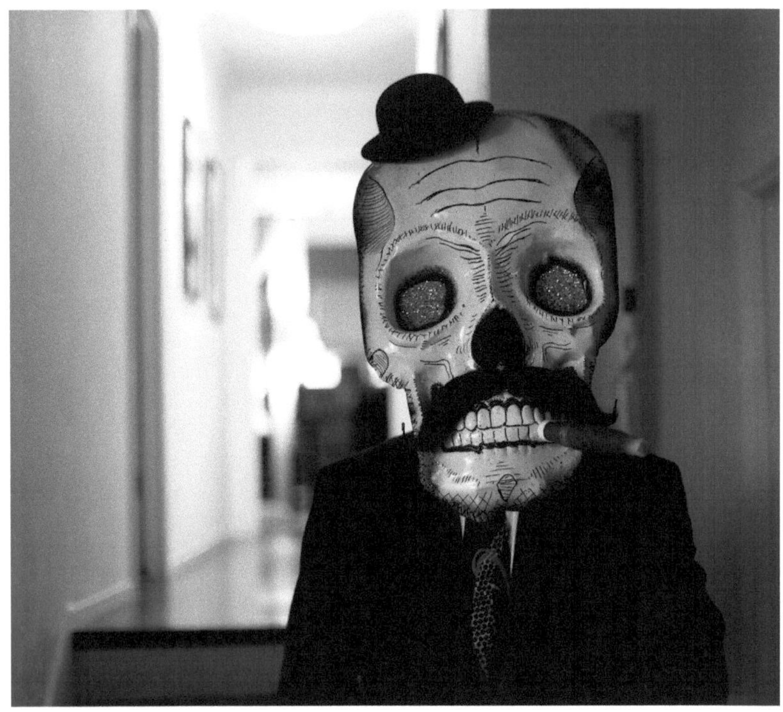

To make a mask that fit like a second skin they first required a mold of my father's ruined face. I sat in a green vinyl chair and watched them work while he breathed through a rubber hose. This was after midnight in an office above a bowling alley.

The woman spooned thick white gook from a glass bowl onto my father's cheeks and forehead. She wore a nurse's uniform. Her pink eyeglasses hung on a chain. She plopped the stuff on, and the man helped spread it flat with a wide stick. Both of them wore white rubber gloves and paper surgical masks.

"Keep those big baby blues closed now," the woman said.

"Not so tight you create lines," said the man.

"No squinting," said the woman.

Through his tube my father made kazoo sounds like he was laughing.

"Please don't move," the man said. "We want to avoid unnecessary impressions."

The woman worked at scraping the bowl while the man used his stick to smooth paste over my father's scars.

"How you doing in there? You doing okay?" the man said. He worked the stick slow and steady.

The woman blinked at me. "We should do the boy."

"Why," said the man.

She wrinkled her nose beneath her mask. "He's too pretty."

My father joined his hands behind his neck. He looked comfortable with his feet up. I listened for his breathing.

"This won't take long, sweetie," the woman said. "There's a soda machine out in the hall. You don't need any money for it."

While the white gook dried on my father's face, the man and woman stood by an open window and smoked from the same cigarette.

I wandered into another office, turned lights on, found a *Highlights* magazine and flipped to the hidden picture. I studied it awhile. Then I undid two buttons and slipped the magazine inside my shirt, tucking it into the waistband of my jeans. I looked around for other things I could take back to the motel.

"Button your shirt," my father said.

He had a drink in his hand. His hair was sticking up rooster style. He stared at me like I was a stranger. "What are you doing in here?" His face looked raw, like new sunburn. A wormy scar connected his mouth to his ear where it intersected a wavy scar that cut beneath his eye. "What are you hiding?"

"Nothing," I said.

He looped one arm around my waist, scooped me up and carried me on his hip. In the hallway we passed the man and woman who were talking quietly by the soda machine.

While his new face was cooking, stinking up the room, he held me on his jittering knee, his big hand squeezing the magazine against my ribs. He sipped his drink and told me again about Saint Louis, about the Gateway Arch, about our chances of finding my mother there. He promised we would never stop searching.

But really we were moving further away all the time. ■

My Daily Bread

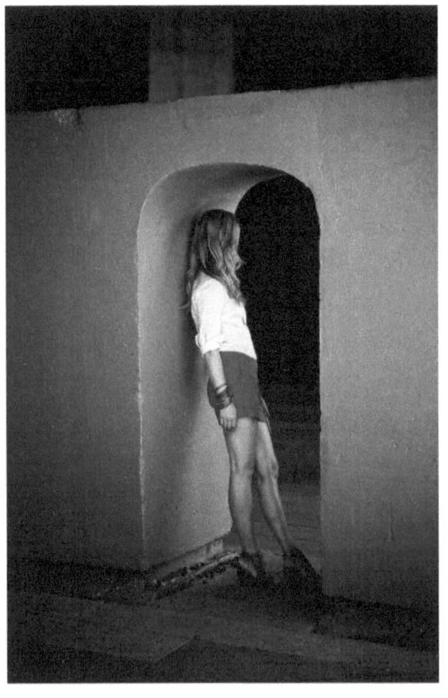

My father came home from the dog track with the big news of the week: I just nailed Nicki Lawrence, he said, pulling a beer from the fridge.

Nicki Lawrence was our ex-neighbor and my former babysitter. Her local claim to fame was she'd once marched in a Macy's Christmas parade with rainbow ribbons tied to the ends of her long braids. I'd had a crush on her since kindergarten.

Where? How? I said.

Just now.

He twisted the cap from the bottle; beer foamed out over his hand.

Picked her up over on the east side, right outside Peabody's. She was hawking with a bunch of whores.

He licked at the foam.

You want one?

I shook my head.

Plainville was a bust, my father said. I hate the dogs. Why do I go?

I don't know, I said.

Please, he said. Don't let me bet dogs anymore. Please. They're too unstable.

Okay, I said.

I mean it. I'm done with the hounds. Dogs and soccer suck. Forget 'em. From now on I'm strictly horses and football.

Tell me about Nicki, I said.

He tilted the bottle to his lips and arched his back until the bottle was almost straight up. I watched him drink. He didn't have a job, didn't work, but his sports jacket reeked of sweat. I watched his throat move like mice were running down it.

You wouldn't have known her, my father said. Looks twice her age.

Years back, when the Lawrences broke apart, Nicki had run. Her mom stuck around for a month, then moved to a safe house across the river. For years I had held to a fantasy that Nicki would come back looking for her mom and she'd find me waiting on the front porch. I'd sometimes gaze out my window across the way at the lot where their building had been. I'd smoke a cigarette and stare and practice waiting.

My father belched. Half the beer was gone.

And she's on something, he said. Definitely. You can tell by her eyes. Nothing left to her. Still pretty, though. All boobs and bones. But her face has that classic structure. She certainly grew up to be a pretty little whore.

What's she look like?

Bleached blonde hair and raw eyes. Two gypsy rings pierced above her eyebrow, which I didn't like. But she knew me, all right. Called me Pete. She remembered me at a glance. Came over to the car and leaned in. Big bubble gum pink lips smirking and grinning. Pete, Pete, Pete, she said. How you doing, Pete, she said. She always had such nice even teeth.

Oh yummy, who's this now who knows me, I thought to myself.

She leaned her head in and shook my hand like we were meeting at church. She asked about you, and had we heard from your sister, and how we were managing, just us two, and wasn't it a shame about families. She slid into the front seat and we talked and I mentioned your mother, whose death she'd heard about, and she started to cry, just a little, maybe a tear or two, and that touched me so I gave her twenty dollars and took her around the corner and bounced her on my lap for half an hour then dropped her off.

Where?

In an alley, parked between two dumpsters. I fucked her slow with the air conditioning on high. She tried to hurry me by wiggling her ass and kissing my ear, but I got my money's worth. Remember what a cock tease that bitch used to be.

I watched him drink.

Where did you drop her off?

Across from Saint Mary's church. She ran into a hole in a fence around a condemned building. Said she could make a wholesale buy from a discount dealer. She asked me to wait and I promised her I would and bring her back to the east side, but after about five minutes of idling gasoline I wasn't going to sit between a church and a condemned building waiting for some whore. I know what you're thinking. Go on. Take a ride. You might find her walking. You got money?

I shook my head no.

Take a twenty, my father said. She'll go again.

He presented a crisp bill.

Go on. My treat. Go ahead. Do her once for yourself.

I said, Okay. And took the twenty.

Now, hey. Don't waste that money, my father said. That's part of your next birthday present.

I didn't say anything. My birthday wasn't for another five months. I'd be gone by then.

And tell her who you are, my father said. Look her right in the eyes. Then fuck her silly. Fuck her like you mean it.

I'll try, I said.

Remember how you worshipped her when she would babysit your ass. Remember how snide she could be with your mother. Like her family was better than ours. Remember how she tickled your belly until you pissed all over your Easter outfit.

I remember, I said.

Good. Don't forget any of that. It's all important.

I started down the stairs.

Don't stay out too late.

Don't worry about me, Dad, I said.

Hell, that's all I worry about. That's all of it. That's everything, my father said. ■

Not The Real Jesus Christ

In no time my father worked himself up to phone privileges. He'd been back in Butler's Psychiatric Hospital less than a month.

"Well, I'm calling," he said. "Guess that makes me a big fat liar."

This was Sunday, during dinner, exactly two weeks since I'd seen him last. At that time he weighed less than one hundred pounds and had threatened to permanently punch my lights out the next time he laid eyes on me. I'd been keeping tabs on his status by checking in daily with the hospital's switchboard.

I said, "Dad! You're hardly fat." And I carried the phone back to my liver and onions.

At the ringing phone, Joan hadn't flinched. Now she glared at me from what had become her side of the dinette table, where our daughter's high chair was set kittty-corner. Leslie was giving Joan a hard time about swallowing mashed peaches and pears.

"Just because I'm calling" my father said. "Don't think I forgive you. Because that's not the case. You had no right and no business bringing me back here."

"Hey. I'm glad you called," I said cheerfully.

"Find out what he wants," Joan said.

"They took me off feedings," my father said. "Don't sound like much, I know, but it's a big step around here."

"What am I supposed to do," I hissed at Joan.

"You know my position," Joan said.

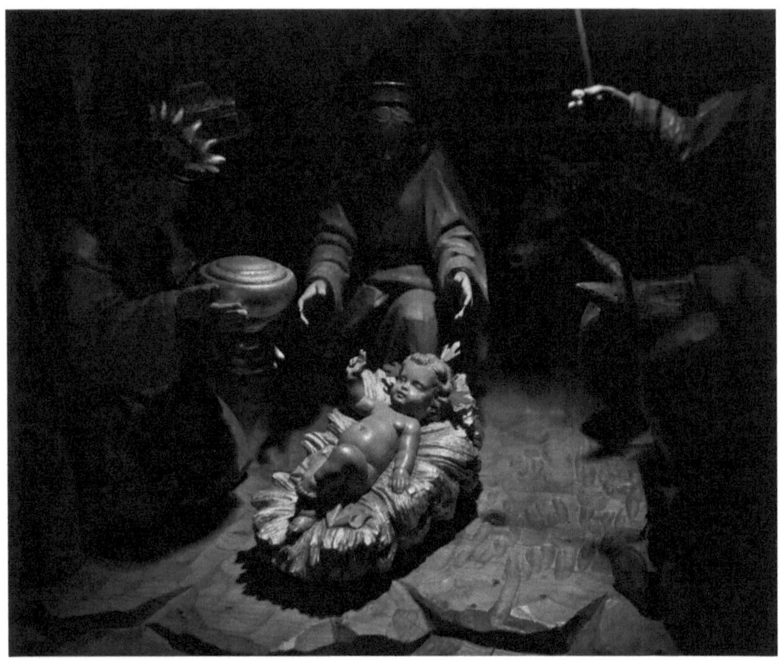

"They're still pumping me full of god knows what, but at least I keep my meals down, and I don't shit my pants, so they let me roam around like I own the place."

Joan starred at me, bug eyed, slack jawed.

"I still miss your mother, the old witch. I still talk to her, but only after lights out, before I drift off. And I don't tell anyone she answers me, because when you're honest with people around here they whistle like you're the triangle in the percussion section."

He'd been grieving nearly a year, in and out of Butler's twice since my mother died. "You sound a lot better," I said.

"Screw how I sound. My goddamn hands won't stop shaking. And I've got a nasty rash where nobody wants one. They tell me it's the medication, but I know it's something else, some kind of nerve damage."

"I'm sure it's the pills, a side effect."

"You think I'm nuts, don't you?"

"No dad, I don't think that at all."

"I might be," he said. "I'm close. Don't think I don't know the fix I've put myself in."

Joan scooped mush into Leslie's open mouth. "I'm not doing this every time that man decides to come back to earth."

"Is that Joanie, I hear. Tell her I said hello."

"No, that's just the TV," I said, and gave Joan a harsh look. "I'll turn it down."

"Make sure he understands he's not welcome here when he gets out. Not again. We've made our contribution."

"Anyway," my father said, "I woke up this morning thinking that if you're not too busy you might want to drive up and visit. Maybe bring the baby. It's up to you."

"What's he saying," Joan said. "Is he talking about me?"

I shook my head at her.

"I'm not in the same building," my father said. "There's a courtyard here. Bricked-in little garden. If you come up, we could all sit far from the others and the kid wouldn't know the difference from being in a park someplace."

"Sure, dad. We'll drive up for a visit. How 'bout Sunday."

"Don't tell him Sunday," Joan said.

"Sunday?" my father said. "What's today?"

Joan wagged the spoon. "Tell him Sunday isn't good."

"Isn't today Sunday," my father said.

I said, "Hold on a second, dad." And cupped my hand over the phone. "What's wrong with Sunday," I said to Joan.

Leslie said, "Da!"

"Tell him you'll call him back after we talk about it."

"I'm not doing that."

"Well you better tell him something, because we're at my mother's all day Sunday helping with her yard sale."

"Shit," I said.

Leslie said, "Da-da!"

I wiggled my fingers at her. "Hi pretty girl."

Joan banged the spoon to get Leslie's attention. "Go alone," she said. "It's fine."

"What?"

"Go see your father."

"Joan."

"We'll help grandma, and do all daddy's work, and have all our fun without him, won't we sweetie?"

"Joan?"

"You're going to do what you want. So do it."

Into the phone I said. "Dad? You there?"

"Tell him whatever you want, I don't care anymore," Joan said.

"Yup. Still here. Just saying hello to Jesus," my father said.

"Dad? We'll ride up on Sunday."

"Don't say we. Say you," Joan said.

"Not the real Jesus Christ, of course. That's just how this fellow thinks of himself."

I looked at my plate. "So we'll see you on Sunday, then. The three of us."

"No," Joan said.

"We've got two here," my father said. "They're a pair. Each convinced the other Jesus is crazy. They bump in the hall and bless one another. I'll introduce you. Two funny guys."

Joan was still shaking her head very slowly.

"I need to go, Dad. I'll see you Sunday."

"Of course they'll talk your ear off if you stand still long enough. They'll each give you a sermon."

Joan sat silent, gazing at me from a space flatter than any picture.

I looked at my liver and onions. "Dad?"

"Yeah, son?"

"How's today. How's this evening?"

"Today?"

"Joan's busy tonight, she's helping her mom, so it'll be just me and the baby."

"Lie your head off, but you are not taking this baby into a nut house," Joan said.

"Hey you, hey Jesus," my father said. "Guess who's coming to see us? My granddaughter."

Joan hoisted Leslie from her high chair and slung her over her shoulder. The kid looked startled, on the verge of tears. I watched them leave the room. My father was still talking about Jesus, or talking to him, one of them. I looked down at my plate. I picked up my fork and moved the meat around. I remembered how in the days when I refused to eat liver my mother would lie and tell me it was sandwich steak. Just without the sandwich.

"Dad?" I said.

"Yeah, son?"

Leslie began to wail in the other room. In a minute I'd go in and rescue her.

"When I come up," I said, "Maybe we can talk a little about mom. About the kind of person she was."

"Still my favorite topic," my father said.

I told him I'd see him in a half hour, then hung up the phone, suddenly missing my mother, grieving over the fact she'd never laid eyes on her granddaughter. I found Joan pacing with the baby. Leslie was red-faced and screaming.

I put my arms up and clapped my hands.

"Don't even think about it," Joan said.

But I was determined to break her arm if I had to. ■

Dry Socket

NOT QUITE HALFWAY THOUGH THAT TERRIBLE YEAR, WHEN you begin to miss your mother more than ever, your father takes an impromptu break from looking for her. But only because he is recovering from a rotted molar extraction and doesn't have the energy for tracking down a runaway wife. For three days he is deeply despondent because he can't smoke, not even a few puffs of his pipe. Doing so, he has been warned, will dislodge the clot and cause a condition called dry socket, which he has been assured is as intensely painful

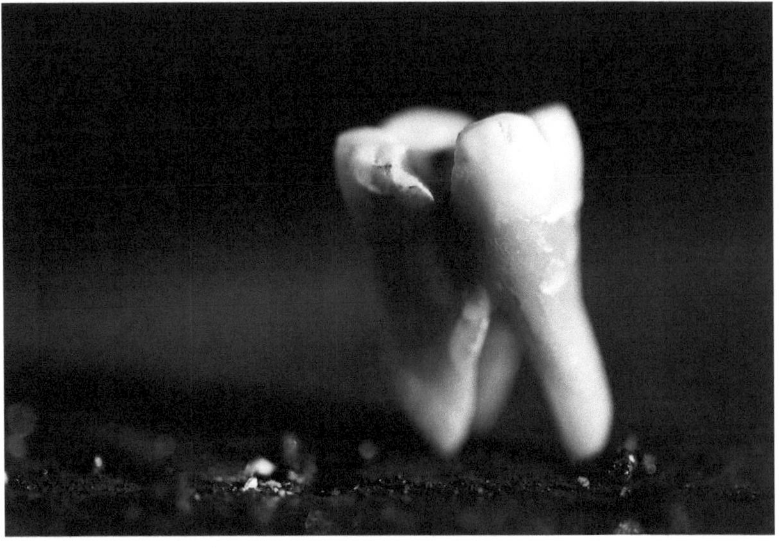

as thirty days in a dungeon during the height of the Spanish Inquisition.

On the fourth day of his recovery, he almost breaks. You're tearing off the page on your word-a-day calendar when you catch him packing his pipe with cherry tobacco, then tapping the stem playfully against his lips. But instead of lighting up, he drinks from a bottle of Grey Goose Vodka, plops in front of the TV, and steadily sips himself blissfully into sleep.

Though you are not the man he is, you decide to go looking for your mother alone, setting out on an unfamiliar path into a part of the forest the two of you have never searched before. You walk for hours, until the sky turns to stone and you feel foolish for bringing nothing along to drink or eat. Without the sun and without your father to guide, you are completely lost. So you backtrack for a while, hoping to find some trace of your own footprints.

Somewhere between a lake and a mountain it begins to snow big flakes that make you forget it is summer; but the ground remembers, refusing to hold a single snowflake longer than a heartbeat. You take the snow as an omen and keep walking in a direction you hope will lead anywhere but straight home.

Invariably, as these things so often turn out, you stumble upon an isolated cottage, though this one has no place being where it is, so close to a cliff that a portion of the foundation and the entire back porch extend over the edge like a diving board.

All the windows are shuttered so you can't peek inside, and when you knock a woman answers the door. She has short hair and big eyeglasses with thick frames. She takes one look at you and says, "Go home before I ruin you. Run along. Shoo!"

Then she retreats, leaving the door wide open, as though inviting you in. She isn't your mother, not even close in age (too young) or shape (too thin) or looks (too plain), but because you still believe in witches you suspect she might be one, then a sign hanging above the fireplace more or less confirms that suspicion. In old English script is printed:

Don't trust in fairly tales
or believe in happy endings.
Hansel and Gretel both died here.

When you inquire if the sign is a joke, she smirks. "Suffice it to say I enjoyed every drop of the thick, sweet broth made from boiling their broken bones. But don't be frightened. Those days are behind me. I promise I won't eat you."

You ask if you can use her phone.

"Where do you think you are," she says.

You explain that you're somewhat lost.

"Somewhat meaning completely," she says, smiling. "I do not apologize for sounding harsh. You're not the first, you know. How old are you?"

"Almost twenty," you lie.

"Really," she says. "I would have guessed older."

Then she laughs, and because you have memorized your mother's laugh, you know this snorting hoot is nothing close to what genuine laughter sounds like.

Nonetheless, you want to bring her home, this woman, this witch, as a gift for your father. Because why not? She has a well-bred manner, a tight smile, and a polite way of seeming pleasantly nasty. It is effective, appealing. You already have an inherent weakness for short-haired women with eyeglasses that make their eyes look enormous. Plus she is dressed like an elementary school teacher in a starched white blouse and a long, form-fitting skirt with crisp pleats that flare out from the waist to her ankle-length hem. She reminds you a little of Miss Plante, your second grade teacher, a shrewish woman whom you once loved with all your heart and gave, for Valentine's Day, a dried starfish into which you had carefully carved your initials. In return, just days later, Mrs. Plante bent at the waist and confided to you and you alone in a mouth to ear whisper that her secondhand penny loafers once belonged to a nun.

"Hungry?" the woman says.

"Famished," you say, reciting this morning's word of the day.

She gives you a bowl with cubed chunks of sweet Virginia ham drowning in honey sauce and raisins. While you eat she pours vinegar on a line of ants marching in tight formation from beneath her refrigerator.

Here, in summary, are the things she tells you:

She once married the wrong man but divorced the right one, and before that she was a seamstress for a wardrobe designer in West Hollywood. She learned the craft from her father who ran a tailor shop called Snip, Pinch n' Tuck before it burned to the ground.

"As a child I used to spend my Saturdays dressing male mannequins in three piece suits then posing them in the front window, though most of my father's clients were filthy rich women, often divorced or widowed, who dressed for fun, or dressed to please, or dressed to kill."

While you listen, you smoke one of her menthol cigarettes and try to look older than you are. She unlatches one of the shuttered windows to let the smoke out. It's dark and there's no moon, and you wonder if your father, alarmed by your absence, is using that worry as a reason to smoke.

"You can stay the night," she says without you asking.

She gives you a short tour of the place. She shows you an emergency exit for redundancies and a window-sized shelf crowded with incoherent elements she calls mementos. She begs to know what questions you can't help asking yourself, and you have plenty of those, but you forgot to bring your list. So you stutter and stammer fully inadequate and incomplete answers, which is to say you speak in hesitations and eccentric rhythms, telling her, basically, nothing at all.

She lets you sleep between her slim curled body and the wall in a bed that is just a mattress on the floor. The air is too hot for a blanket. Sometime during the night you wake up sweating. She wraps her arm plus her leg around you and that makes you come alive. If she knows what she is doing or where it might lead she sure doesn't act like it matters. There is no sweet talk or dirty talk. She has a mole on her breast, and a small pink pimple on one cheek of her ass. Her legs need shaving. They wear you down. You give up early, then she gives up everything until she has pulled from your mouth a sound your throat has never made before.

You wake exhausted after a marathon of dreams too shocking to bear. Shrill bird noises crossing from every direction. You smoke her last two menthols for breakfast and wash the minty taste down with Daffodil tea made from boiled rainwater. She gives you directions that sound too simple to misconstrue, then speaks about her future plans in rapid, broken sentences that on a printed page might align unjustified like staggered steps running down the side of a poem.

A few hours later you are home, where you find your father on his knees, stuffing family photos and a shoe box of love letters into the cold wood stove. He is smoking his pipe, hands free. He closes the little door on the stove then pats his fingers together like he is wiping away dust. "Now all my covert communications shall remain forever undisclosed." Then he says, "Did you find her?"

"No."

"Get lost looking?"

You nod.

"I've done that," he says. "Don't lose hope. Okay?"

You ask how he is feeling. You mean his mouth, his missing tooth.

He says, "Lately I have this overwhelming sense that I'm dying, which of course I am, and quite naturally, though far more rapidly than previously planned." He puffs his pipe, but no smoke comes out. "How 'bout you," he says. "How's my big, beautiful boy doing today?"

But you don't know where to begin, how to end, what the middle might be. And for a few heartbeats, even motherless, you're happy enough without any explanation for your happy, bitter heart. ■

What Are the Odds?

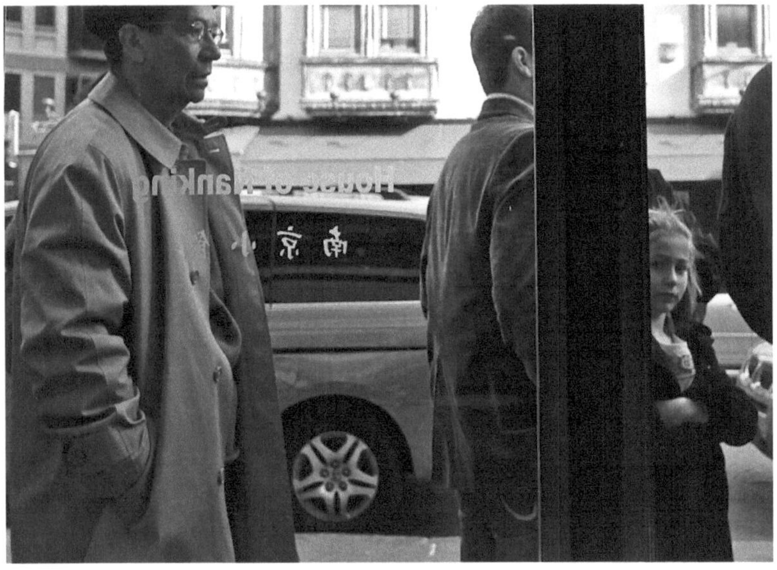

THE ONLY PHOTO I HAVE OF LILLY SHOWS THREE WINDOWS above three rose bushes by a chain link fence and, of course, Lilly, more or less centered, though slightly out of focus. My own shadow—a sharp silhouette of a fool wearing a fedora and holding a camera—partially obscures her face, so you can't see that the hue of her lipstick that June day was as dark as the rose petals scattered around her feet. But what you can see are her eyes, two black holes, like apertures about to snap open and swallow me whole.

Entirely by chance and without premeditation by either party, the young beauty had become the last frame in a roll of 35mm self-portraits I was preparing for a class I was teaching. I'd spent half the day strolling the east side, seeking my own reflection in shop windows and car windshields, in ditch water and shards of broken glass.

How it happened that I ran into Lilly was that I had simply arrived at a spot I sometimes walk to, and Lilly, who had skipped her classes that day, strolled by on her way from one place to someplace else. Maybe it was the sun—I had neglected to wear my cap—but I was so delighted to see a familiar face I raised the camera, aimed, and snapped: windows, fence, Lilly and the roses.

That's all, really. No more to it.

Except that her smile made me nervous. Lilly's smile always made me nervous. Mainly because it was almost entirely a tense and uneasy smirk as though she were keeping a secret from no one else but me.

What I am fumbling to say is we knew each other prior to this occasion, though hardly. In truth we were strangers. I had twice seen her strolling the campus, twice noticed her in the cafeteria, and once spotted her front row center at one of my lectures. On the third occasion her legs were crossed high and she was directing her smirk like a spotlight. What I am trying to say is her smile was a wish and a dream. I still can't explain. I still don't understand. What are the odds that any two sets of eyes, hands, mouths, and bodies line up so perfectly, even for one afternoon?

I said to her afterwards, after drinks and more, I said, "I bet when you were painting your face this morning you never dreamed it would end up a rainbow on my pillow."

"You're awfully sure of yourself," she said, reapplying lipstick. "And for the record, that's hardly a rainbow. Merely a smear of misdirected passion." She kissed a tissue to blot her lips. "And I didn't do this, you did. That's a portrait of pure animal lust."

Due to some gross misunderstanding and much to my chagrin, I had apparently taken her the wrong way and too quickly, much like a dumb old dog who buries his bone in the wrong yard without gnawing or even licking it.

My embarrassment aside, now she was offended and painfully sore, with obvious spotting on the rear of her white denim slacks.

I felt silly, of course. I'm rarely prone to such impropriety. To make matters worse she was younger than she appeared; a mere high school senior taking college courses for extra credit.

But I didn't know that then or her well enough to apologize, so I did the next best thing. I escorted her to the bus stop and gave her my last token. We waited a while, quietly. As awkward a moment as I have lived. When the bus came, I watched her get on, and move quickly through to the very last seat. I waited for her to wave through the window. She didn't. So I walked home, concerned less about the incident than about her lack of common decency, the mark, I believe, of an entire generation doomed to misunderstanding its senior members. I put on my slippers, heated water for tea, changed the sheets, tacked the pillowcase to the wall.

It hangs there still. ■

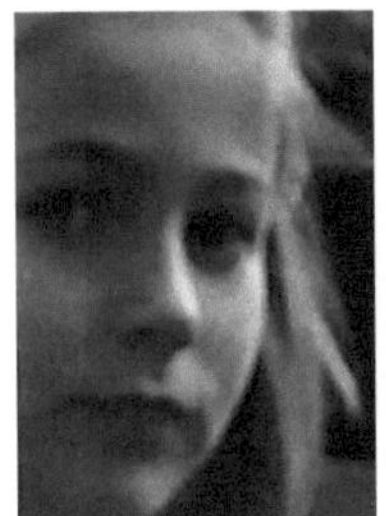 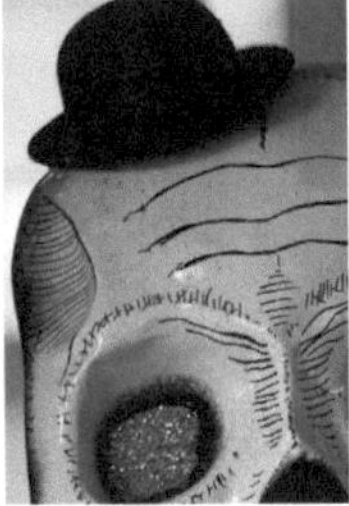 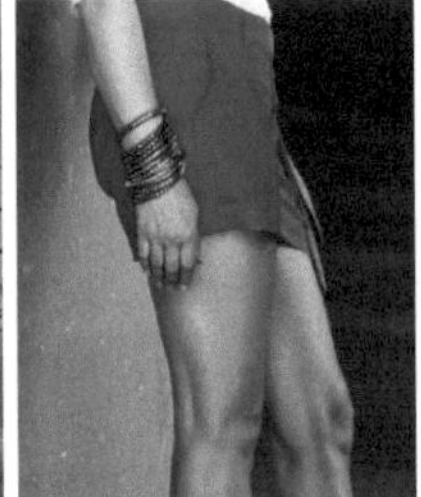 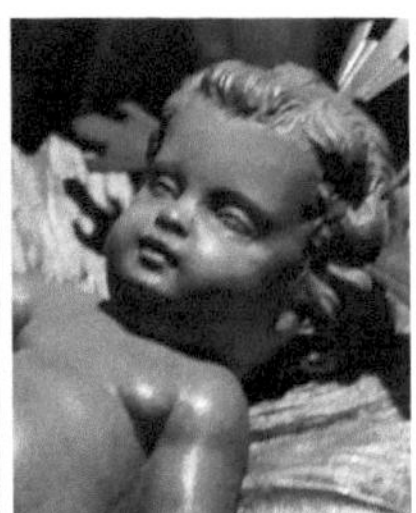

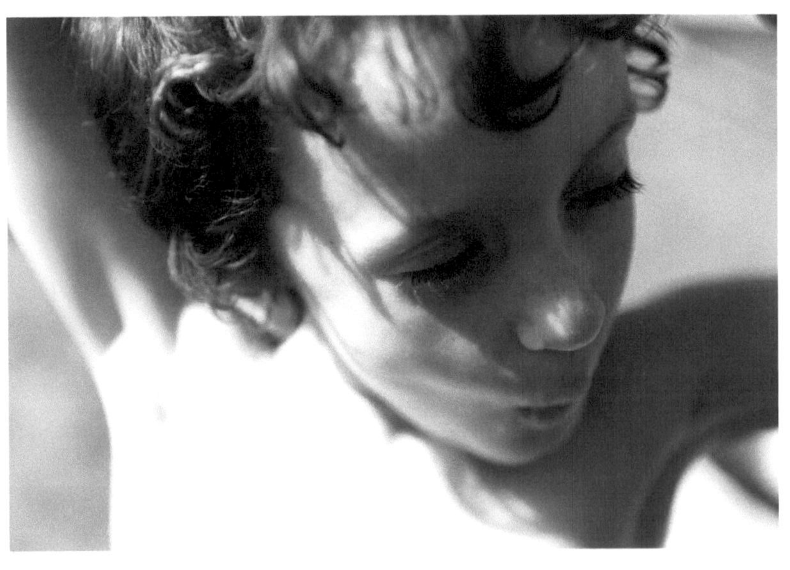

Women and Children

The Baby's Name

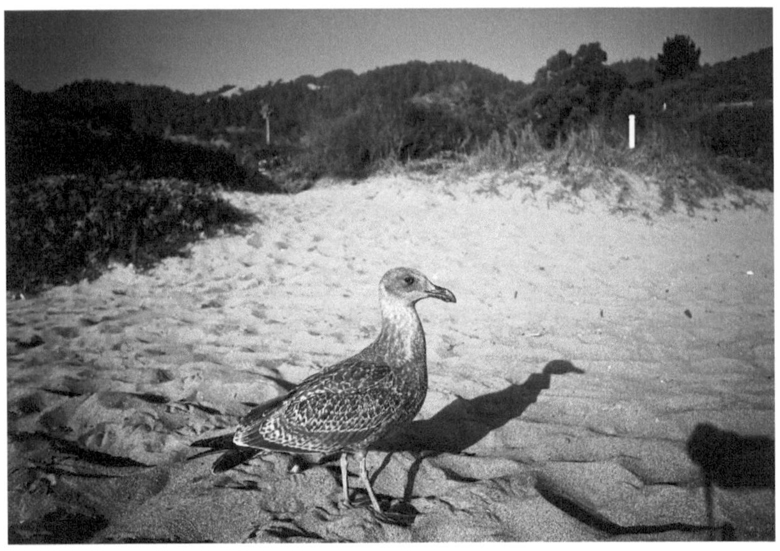

The first screech sounds like some teenaged punk in a hot rod burning rubber. Probably the neighbor's kid, Arthur decides. The second screech could be a chainsaw whining as it knifes through hardwood. What daredevil/fool is working his woodpile at this time of night? The third screech shatters Arthur's sleep into a thousand fragments. He blinks at the darkness, pulls a breath, and resettles. A baby is crying. Whose baby? In a heartbeat he decides the commotion doesn't concern him, and his mind presses back toward sleep, filtering the noise, sorting its layers.

First is night sound, the silence beneath, the dense hush that forms the foundation, blending the whole clamor into one unsettling racket, like a group of incompetent musicians tuning their instruments.

This is not the layer that wakes him.

Second is the familiar raspy grate of his wife's snores. The gush of air from mouth to lungs causes her throat to vibrate. It's not her fault. She's a frail woman with a delicate neck and a narrow airway. In deep sleep her breathing causes the floppy tissues to knock against the back of her throat.

This is not the sound that wakes him.

It's the third layer that unsettles, making sleep hard to hold. The cry is that of an angry cat. A cat with its tail caught in a meat grinder. Someone is slowly but efficiently cranking, pulling the creature in, shredding flesh and fur.

No healthy baby should ever make a sound like that.

The feral shrieks jolt Arthur awake. He blinks again, turns onto his side, disentangles his legs from the top sheet. His brain merges the child's cry into a dream—he's riding a ferry across a choppy sea, holding to the rail at the rear of the ship, watching the baby's crib being tugged by a heavy rope while above her ten or twenty sea gulls glide on arched wings.

Are the birds dangerous? Arthur murmurs.

There are new rules to follow, a long list of procedures. Baby dos-and-don'ts. Rule number one is Arthur must never pick up the child after midnight no matter how hard she cries. Otherwise, she'll never learn.

The muscles in her lower intestines are undeveloped and slow to process. Gas builds up, cramping her with pain. His wife had it. His mother-in-law had it. It's in the genes.

The baby shrieks, a long sustained alto.

Arthur calls her name from the railing of the ship and the wind pushes the sound back into his face. He worries about the sea gulls as the crib rises and falls, riding the white surf. Will they try to pick her up, peck at her flesh, pull away pieces like pink salmon?

The rope is taut, as thick as his arm.

His wife snores.

The baby's name is not the one Arthur picked from the book of names. She has the name his wife and mother-in-law circled in red. It begins with the same letter of the name Arthur decided upon. Holding to the ship's rail, twisting in restlessness, he tries to take comfort in that fact.

Guinevere is the name Arthur wanted. But his mother-in-law said it sounded too much like a black name.

A black name? How is Guinevere a black name, he asked his wife.

Gwen, his wife said. That's what people will end up calling her. Gwen, she hissed. Which is definitely a black name.

His wife snores like a rhinoceros. In the dream she is beside Arthur on the boat, asleep in a deck chair.

Arthur lets go of the railing, jostles her shoulder which is slick with tanning lotion.

The baby, he says.

What baby, his wife says.

Our baby. She's crying, says Arthur.

His wife tips back her floppy hat and glares at the sun, exposing the pale yellow flesh of her face and neck.

Listen, Arthur says. Can't you hear her screams. She must be wet or hungry, or both.

His wife watches the light lose some of its radiance as a cloud slides past.

No. You're wrong, she says. You're dreaming again. It's only the gulls you hear. Those filthy birds have been following us since the ship set sail.

She adjusts her hat and sinks low, hiding her eyes.

Now relax, and enjoy what's left of our honeymoon. Unless you'd prefer to go back to our cabin and make a baby? Your call, she says.

Then the alarm rattles, another day begins, and Arthur sits up, his hands in his hair, his mind filled with the noise that has become his life.

And his daughter cries. ■

Portrait of a Virtuous Woman

Once a week, to startle, to keep Charles alert, I tell the poor bastard I'm getting my hair cut. "Above the ears, chop chop, short as an English schoolboy's."

If Charles looks disinterested, or unusually sedate, or if he seems dulled by my previous threats, I crank up the volume and drill the point home. "Oh, I am serious this time, Charles," and I make scissors of my fingers, snipping

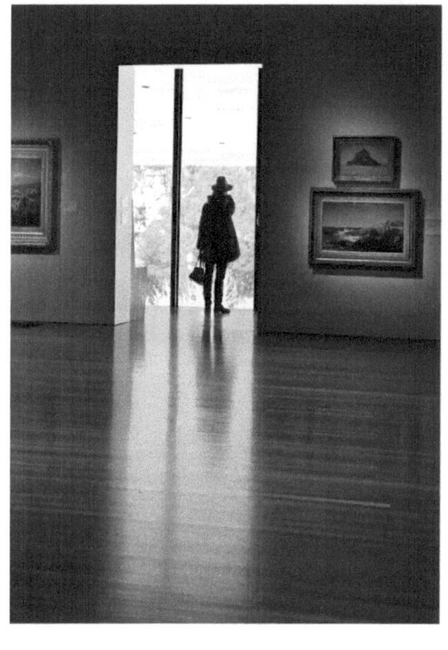

at air. "This time I do mean it, honey. No joke. The appointment has already been made."

I generally carry on as though nothing can stop me. Then I wait and watch my poor husband try.

Not counting split-end trims (half an inch, at most) I have not had my hair cut since I was twelve. That year half my sixth grade class contracted lice, and my mother, as a dumb and unnecessary precautionary measure, cropped my waist-length hair to my jaw. My hair is naturally thick and unnaturally springy, what some men have called wild, and most women call kinky—a term I despise. My mother hated the fight my hair gave her that night. First she couldn't find a pair of scissors that would cut more than a few strands at a time. So she brought out my father's straight razor. He was long gone and the razor, which folded up into a bone handle and reminded me of Jack the Ripper, served no purpose. She plopped a metal mixing bowl on my head and ordered me to hold it still. She sliced a section at a time, working the razor like a saw, while sidestepping her way around the kitchen chair where I sat holding my breath and my tears. I remember the harsh sound of the razor against my hair. I expected each slice to be painful, and it was. Each tug hurt. I felt I was being punished for something I had no part in, and the silence of my mother hurt in a way I cannot begin to describe.

The result, captured in that year's school picture, resembled, at worst, a mushroom, and at best, a bikers' safety helmet set slightly askew. That portrait sat for years on the family TV, but was later lost, along with the bone handled razor and so much other memorabilia, in the fire that destroyed my mother's home and took her life; but I still have a wallet-size photo which I bring out to terrorize Charles when he dares play with the idea that short hair might make me look fashionably sexy. He doesn't say this aloud, of course. A stroke, suffered just before his fortieth birthday, prevents him from forming all but the crudest sounds. But his eyes glisten when he thinks of sex, and the strong side of his mouth, the side that still works, opens and closes, stretching gobs of spittle into a thin white web.

When I see that web begin to form, I know what Charles is thinking, and I bring out the photo and steady it inches from his nose. "Is this what you want," I shout. "Because this is what I'll look like."

Of course I don't need to shout. There's nothing wrong with Charles' hearing, which the stroke left intact, and, if anything, has sharpened over the years. I'm not a cruel person, but I do enjoy a good shout. The whole point of living in the country is the ability to talk at the top of one's lungs and not hear a reply. I adore the silence that is Charles, the quiet man he's become, but I abhor his stubbornness. My hair is a valuable bargaining chip, a part of me that he still holds dear, so I use it to move his mind, to zap a reminder that everything in life can be altered, changed in a matter of seconds, mutated beyond belief, just as he was altered.

Charles has problems with anger. Always has. But lately he'll shake less, twist his head away, fumble with the wheel grip, and try to move himself forward or back. It's pathetic to watch. When I leave the room I lock his wheels.

"It doesn't matter to me either way, Charles. I only see myself in the mirror a few minutes each day. You'll have to look, you'll have to live with a short-haired woman. Is that what you want? Is it, Charles?"

No matter what it is I'm trying to persuade him to do—eat, drink, bathe, swallow his medication—he'll consent. No fuss. No tears. No more anguished deep-throated howls. He becomes a child, a little boy accepting my good judgment.

Thirty-five years ago, when Charles proposed, I made him admit that it was my hair he loved most about me. Layered cuts and rag styles were in vogue then. Most of my friends had waves of pin curls. I toyed with the idea of changing my look, of shortening or thinning my mop. But a young Marine named Charles convinced me that long flowing hair was the mark of a virtuous woman, a superior breed of female unashamed to stand apart from the crowd. When I argued that long hair made me feel old-fashioned, he said, "And what is wrong with that? God and Country are old-fashioned too, but I'm not about to give them up."

He was a Private First Class Marine and proud of it. I liked him more than any man or boy I had dated, but I didn't want to marry him. When he proposed I was flattered, but I didn't love him and I didn't want him—and I wouldn't, not really, for a long time after. So I answered, as I had been instructed to answer all questions—politely, with virtue and grace.

I said, "No thank you, Charles."

Said it plain and flat as vanilla, just as if I were turning down a sweet, or a cigarette, or an invite to a movie I had already seen.

At the end of that summer, Charles left for Viet Nam. And I went to secretarial school. mainly because I had been told it was what smart pretty girls did after high school. Within days of Charles' departure, a man I typed letters for tried to French kiss me, and I chipped his molar with my ring. So he fired me. That night I wrote Charles. And I did a very stupid thing. I swore an oath, a pledge of allegiance and faith, a sacred promise to remain as virtuous and true as I was pretty. To Charles, for always, to him and him alone, I keep that promise. No one has yet dared try to make me stop. ■

Lost and Found

I LOST MY PRETTY MOTHER IN A TOY STORE. ENTIRELY MY fault. Despite her usual warnings, I wandered, I strayed. Up one aisle, down the next. I became so bewitched by the dolls and accessories that only after an hour did I turn myself in.

I was a lanky thing—all limbs, lace, and hair.

A hefty clerk boosted me by my hips onto the service desk. His name-tag read: CARL.

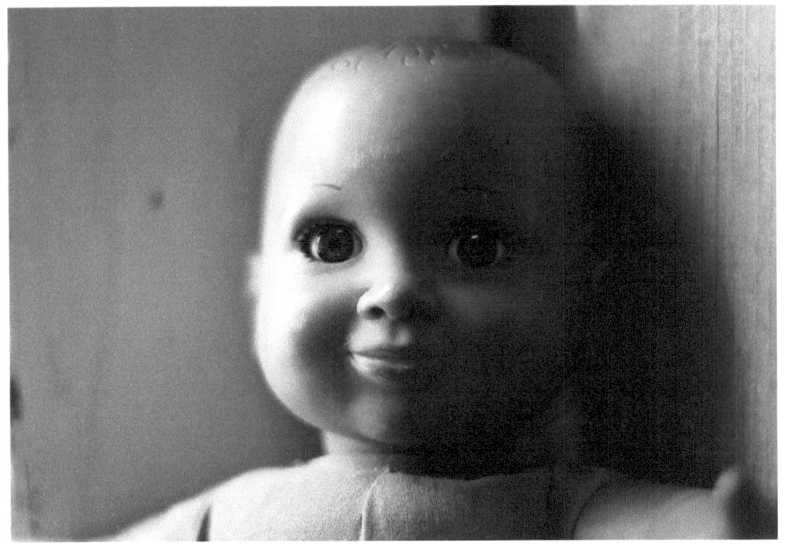

Above our heads hung a sign on a chain: LAYAWAYS & RETURNS.

"What's your name, sweetheart," Carl said.

He had a clipboard with a pencil on a string.

"Last name first, first name last," said Carl.

But I had been taught to ignore the inquiries of strangers. So I played dumb, content to gaze and click my heels.

Carl looked me over, up and down, up and down, then jotted a few words on his clipboard. He told me to "wait right there," so I crossed my legs and waited.

Within minutes the store manager, a short ugly man with a patch of thinning hair, handed me an ice-cold bottle of Coke.

"What do you say," he said.

He wanted a thank you, but I'd seen him fetch the soda using keys to the machine so it hadn't cost him a dime.

"What's your mother look like, kid?"

"She's tall," I said. "Tall as a tree."

"What color hair?"

"Foxy blonde, streaked with grey."

"Pretty?"

"Head to toe," I said.

"How old?"

"Me or her?"

"Let's stick with her."

"Agelessness is her secret," I said.

"Approximately," he said.

I sipped the Coke: "Do the math. Three times me."

"Okay, then. How old are you, honey?"

"Guess," I said.

He shook his head, showing his yellow teeth.

"Bet you can't guess," I said, and stuck out my tongue.

"Bet what? With what will you bet?"

"Bet you another Coke," I said.

He guessed wrong four times in a row. I giggled after guesses three and four. The fool was going higher, not lower.

"Hey," he said. "Did you really lose a mother, or is this some type of scam?"

I squeezed my face, closed my eyes. I made myself ugly and started to cry. I kicked and banged my heels until both my shoes flew off. A lady customer looked my way. "What's that child fussing about," she said.

Carl the clerk said, "I forget her story. Will that be cash or charge, ma'am?"

I screamed a terrific scream, a howl that would make any mother proud. I screamed so hard I hurt my throat. So loud the clerk punched out and went home.

Not entirely my fault. It was closing time anyway.

The ceiling lights went dark in rows. The ugly manager jiggled his keys to get my attention. He had my shoes hooked on the ends of his fat fingers. He strolled over and set them on my lap.

"Pretty legs," he said.

All night the ice-cold Cokes slid down my throat like kittens down a well. ■

A Volunteer from the Audience

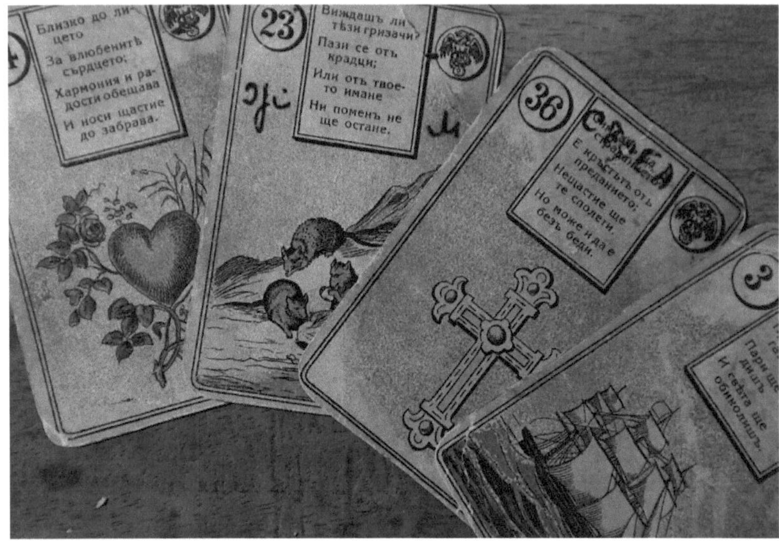

THERE WERE A DOZEN WINDOWS AT STREET LEVEL, AND though their shades were up, the school's auditorium was dark, all the seats empty except for two some twenty or thirty rows back. There, in the murky shadow of the mezzanine, sat my sister Diana and her boyfriend Larry. I was thankful I couldn't see them more clearly. Larry was a pimply, unshaven mess, six weeks out of rehab, and Diana, at seventeen, was bone thin, sickly pale, and five months pregnant.

I stepped onto the stage and walked straight to my sister's customary spot, directly across from my father. My legs were trembling. My mother smiled up at me from her black lacquered box. Only her head and feet were showing.

She said, "Don't be nervous honey." Her face was thick with makeup. The heavy streaks of silver-blue eye shading contrasted with the bright candy-apple red of her lipstick.

My father cleared his throat. He wasn't in costume. His tux and top hat were still at the dry cleaners. Even out of uniform, the seriousness of his expression put a dull ache in my belly.

"Hold on a minute. Nostril itch," my mother said and tightened her face as though preparing to sneeze. "Bobby, scratch beneath my nose for me."

I liked that her arms were trapped inside in the box.

I looked at my father. "She's got an itch. What do I do," I said.

"Nothing," my father said. "Put your shoulders back. Stand up straight. Eyes on me." He presented the two-handled saw across the oblong box.

"Would you be so kind as to examine the teeth for sharpness," he said in a booming voice.

As I reached toward the blade, he jerked the saw back.

"Whoa. Not so fast, son."

"Remember he's a volunteer," my mother said.

"You can't just grab at it," he said. "There's nothing phony about these teeth. They're pure steel."

"Just walk him through it, Frank," mother said. "He'll catch on quick enough."

"I am walking him through it, Lois. I'm doing exactly that."

"He's seen the act a thousand times. He knows it by heart. Don't you Bobby?"

I nodded at my mother.

"Lois, you're distracting him."

"I'm not distracting anyone," my mother said and knocked twice from inside the box.

"Okay. Once more," my father said. He cleared his throat. "Remember this saw is real. Very, very real. You could slice off a finger if you just swipe at it."

I nodded.

"It's made of tungsten," he continued. "NASA makes nozzles for rocket engines from tungsten steel. Did you know that?"

"Fix your tie," my mother said. "Frank, help him with his tie."

"His tie is fine, Lois."

"It's not fine. The knot is askew. The whole thing's hanging cockeyed."

My father studied me for a moment. "She's right. Fix your tie," he said.

I tugged and straightened the knot.

"Oh. Much better. So handsome," my mother said. "You're doing a wonderful job, isn't he Frank?"

My father let out his breath then presented the saw again.

"Careful now. Go slow. Move your finger above the blade, not on it, but close enough so it looks like you're actually touching it. Okay, son?"

"You can't be calling him son when we're on stage, Frank."

Father set the long saw on top of the box. "Lois. Please."

"I'm sorry, Frank, but I think if we're going to rehearse, we should do it the right way."

"He's an eleven-year-old boy. It doesn't mean anything if I call him son. People use that term all the time, on stage and off, so I think I can say son and not have everyone in the audience think 'oh, my, he must be calling him that because they're related.'"

"Don't lecture me, Frank. Not in that tone. I'm uncomfortable enough in this coffin."

"Okay, son," my father said, lifting the saw. "Would you please be so kind as to tell the audience your opinion of the teeth on this saw blade."

I opened my mouth to speak.

"Turn and face the audience," my father said.

"Who are you telling to turn? Not me, I hope," said my mother.

"Lois, please. Can we get through this one time?"

My mother opened and closed her eyes. Her lipstick made her sly grin appear malicious.

"All the way around. That's it. Turn and face the audience," my father said.

I started to speak then reached back for the saw's handle.

"No. Not with the saw. I keep that."

I turned to where in a few hours a paying audience would be seated. It wouldn't be a big audience; they never were. Still, my stomach felt like a nest of angry snakes as I tried to focus. Way back in the shadows Larry had his arm around my sister.

"Frank? Are we nearly through here?" my mother said. "My back is knotting up, and I can't feel my toes."

My father said, "Hold on, wait a second. He's doing it again." I felt his hand on my shoulder. "What is it, son? What do you see out there?"

My German grandmother, who founded the family business after she immigrated to America, had been a capable fortune teller all her life, and, through no fault of my own, I could at odd and awkward moments envision the future of my family. I seldom liked these revelations. As usual, I held my breath and closed my eyes. I saw my sister's face unnaturally colored, her hair delicately arranged on a pink satin pillow, her expression lifeless.

"It's not good," I said. ■

The Stray

ONE SATURDAY, ABOUT ELEVEN MONTHS AFTER OUR MOTHER died, I found my brother behind the garage, shirtless, his feet tangled in the garden hose. He was badly sunburned and oozing blood from a million tiny scratches on his chest and arms. Nearby was a silver-gray tabby, licking itself, half curled on a beach towel. It was an adult cat, mangy and thin. My first thought was to just walk away. But I was already an accomplice; Dad had put me in charge of the little retard.

Though my brother couldn't tie his own shoelaces, he'd somehow managed to bathe, shampoo, and double-knot a pink ribbon around the cat's scrawny neck. He had already named the damn thing. Socks. Short for Socrates.

All he really needed me for was to paint iodine on his wounds, then march inside and ask the big question: "Hey Nora, can we keep an ugly stray Andy found?"

I didn't have the heart to tell him he was bleeding for nothing.

Andy broke into stuttering: "She likes you ba-better. Sa-say, sa-say you fa-found it."

I was a year older, but no less afraid of our new stepmother, a chunky Irish woman Dad had hired to help with laundry and ironing after Mom stopped getting out of bed.

I got Andy to stop picking at his wounds and listen while I rattled off reasons why Nora would say no and why Dad wouldn't overrule her. But you can't talk sense to a twelve-year-old. Especially one who had popped into life feet-first, a deadly shade of blue. Grandma said Andy's umbilical cord had twisted around his neck, blocking oxygen flow to his brain. The right word was "delayed." I'd gotten into fistfights when people called him anything else.

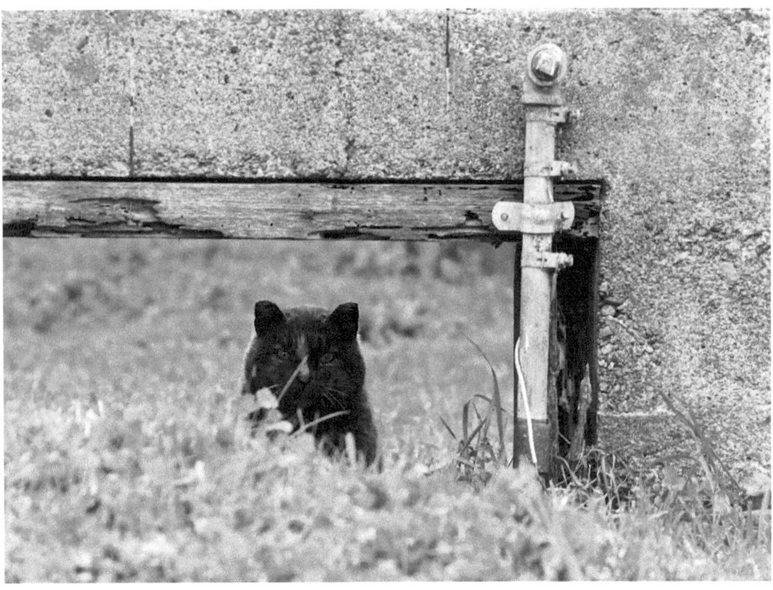

My plan was don't ask and don't tell and see how far that takes us. Together we smuggled Socks into our room through a window. We fixed a box of sand for it to piss in. There were a few close calls but we kept the animal hidden for weeks. We fed it tuna fish and table scraps. It stopped hissing at us and gradually put on weight.

My guess is Nora was snooping, not cleaning, the morning Socks surprised her. Her shriek woke me. I shot out of bed in time to see her use her broom like a hockey stick to swat Socks into a wall.

Then Andy was screaming as loud as Nora. Dad stomped in. He cornered the cat and trapped it with a blanket. "Get a pillow case," he said. "Hurry up."

He stuffed Socks inside and twisted the top into a knot.

"Get in the car, both of you!"

Still in our pajamas, we drove the shaded back road down to the reservoir. Socks rode in the trunk. On the way Dad talked about rabies and fleas and how he was going to teach us "proper procedure" so we'd know what to do if we came across another stray.

Near the water he added a few rocks to give the sack weight, but he must not have knotted it very well because seconds after it hit the water the pillowcase unraveled. As it sank, Socrates paddled toward the opposite shore.

"Look! He can swim," Andy said.

I jabbed an elbow into his side, but it was too late. Dad had already turned to see the cat cutting the surface.

"Swims good," I said.

"Like a rat," my father said. He gripped the rail, poised like he was planning to jump in.

Andy whistled though his teeth. "This way, Socks. Turn around. We're over here."

Dad clamped his big hand on Andy's shoulder, which put a cringe on my brother's face. Though I don't think the hand was meant for anything except to keep Andy from falling in.

The three of us crowded against the rail and watched Socks climb onto the opposite shore, then leap-hop into the woods.

"Goodbye," Andy said.

I thought about my father's .22 in the trunk and how he could nail that cat running full tilt through heavy brush. Then I watched my father's eyes to see if he was thinking that, too.

Andy kept waving a pathetic little baby wave, looking like he was about to burst into tears.

"It's God's cat, now," Dad said and started back toward the car.

"Goodbye Socks," Andy said, still against the rail.

He didn't look like he was going anyplace, so I stretched my neck and spit into the water to check the current. I leaned until I could see my face reflected in the water. I wondered how deep the pillowcase had sunk.

"Nora's waiting," our father said. Then he said, "Quit pressing against that rail before God takes you too."

I stepped away but Andy stayed put. "We're leaving, retard."

While my head was turned the little brat sucker-punched me. My ear throbbed. I thought I'd been stung by a bee, then I figured it out. I swung at him and missed. He took off running, whimpering like a wounded hound.

"Where's he going?" my father said. "Andy!" he called. "The car's this way, son." Then he shook his head at me. "Don't stand there like an idiot. Grab him before he falls into a well and breaks an ankle."

I tried to focus on which way he was pointing.

"Move your feet, boy. Last thing Nora needs is anything on crutches yelping to be soup fed."

But I just stood there rubbing my ear and gazing at a wrinkle of sunlight playing on the water. Maybe it was my brother's sucker-punch, or some small defect in me, or something to do with missing my mother so much, but for nearly a minute I couldn't decide if the old man meant for me to bring back Andy, chase down the cat, or retrieve some part of something else that had somehow gotten away from him. ■

Wooden Matches

RAIN PEPPERED THE WINDOWS OF THE RENTED BEACH HOUSE. The boy sat with his mother who hugged him from behind. Together they watched the storm roll in. Heavy surf crashed into the shoreline and lightning flashes splintered the dark sky.

When the houselights flickered, the boy stiffened.

"Mommy?"

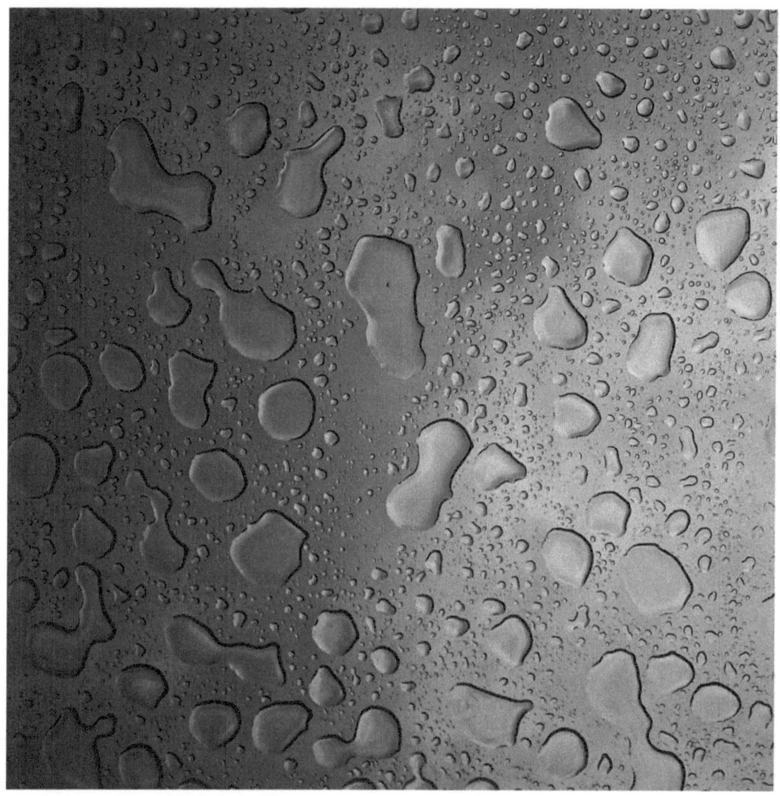

There was genuine panic in his voice.

"Hush," his mother said, and squeezed him about the waist. "Watch the pretty sky."

Thunder rolled and boomed.

Each time the thunder broke, she ruffled the boy's hair or kissed his neck.

Across the room on the couch lay the stepfather, flat on his back, his face turned away.

A tremendous boom rumbled through the house and the lights dimmed. After a long moment the lights grew bright again. The mother released the boy. She went to the kitchen, to her stove. She struck a wooden match on the side of its box. The instant the flame flared the power failed.

"Mommy!"

"Not so loud. I'm right here. See?"

Her face shown above the flame. From across the room the boy watched. All her movements seemed slow and orchestrated as she lit one candle then another using the same match.

Shadows played, shadows loomed.

"Mommy?"

"I'm here, sweetheart."

"Mommy?"

"One second, dear."

The box of matches in hand, she drew the boy away from the window.

"Don't be frightened, now," she said. "There's absolutely nothing to be afraid of." She rested her arms on his small shoulders.

As she hugged him, the boy focused on the stepfather.

Sudden wind shook the house.

Her mouth at his ear, the mother instructed the boy to align four candles in four tin holders. Then she showed him the proper way to strike a match.

"Away. Watch me. Away from your face," she said.

She struck a match then instantly blew out the flame.

The boy nodded, eager to try.

"And never if I'm not here."

The boy reached for the box.

"Never ever," she said.

The boy wiggled his fingers.

"Not yet. First repeat what I said."

"Away from my face," said the boy.

"What else?"

"Never if you're not here."

"And you mustn't tell. Not anyone. Not ever. Promise?"

The child nodded.

"Because you-know-who wouldn't like it. Not one bit."

The child looked at the sleeping man and said, "I won't tell."

The mother pantomimed striking a match, then raised her eyebrows at the boy as she handed him the box. "Careful now."

The boy's hands trembled.

"Close the box before striking," she said.

The boy tried, and failed. He tried again and failed. Several burnt and broken matches later, the storm seemed to stall. Rain stopped assaulting the windows. A softer thunder rumbled without booming. On the couch, the stepfather coughed into his shadow.

The boy squeezed between his mother and the wall. He guided her hands, pushing at her fingers, twisting them to create overlapping shadow puppets that moved above the sleeping man.

"Quack quack," the mother said

"Quack quack," echoed the boy.

"So who's telling our story today?"

The boy shrugged. After a moment he said: "Daddy!"

"Which daddy?"

"My real daddy," the boy said.

"No, no," said the mother. "Better if Little Duck tells this story. See Little Duck? He loves his mama so much he's telling her a wonderful story."

"No," the boy said, squirming. "You tell it. You."

"Keep still," his mother said. She hooked her arm around his waist and held tight.

"You're hurting," the boy said.

"I'm not hurting you. No one is hurting you," she said sharply. Then she loosened her grip. "Today Little Duck is telling our story."

The boy wiggled and squirmed.

"No," he said and made a shadow that ate his mother's long fingers. He watched her eyes as Little Duck chewed. "You tell it," he said. "You! Not Little Duck. You!"

She shifted her position. "Listen to me." She was staring at the sleeping man. "You tell this story. You and Little Duck. You're better at telling."

"What about him," the boy asked.

On the couch the stepfather made no sound.

"Don't worry," she whispered. "If he moves, I'll nudge. I'll warn you the second I hear him stir."

After a moment the boy began, “Once there was a baby duck with two daddies, one good daddy and one very bad daddy.”

“Wait,” the mother said. “Which is which?”

“Ask Little Duck,” said the boy. “He can see in the dark. He knows all my secrets.” ■

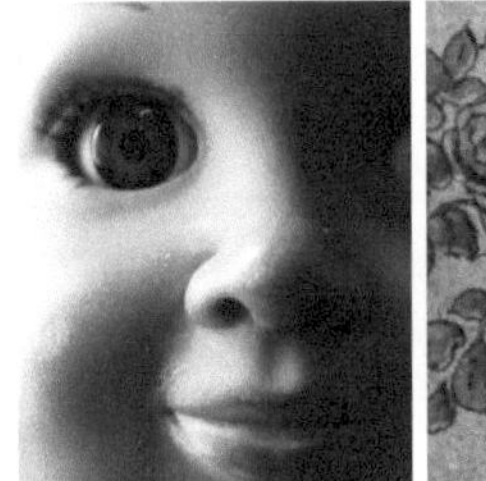 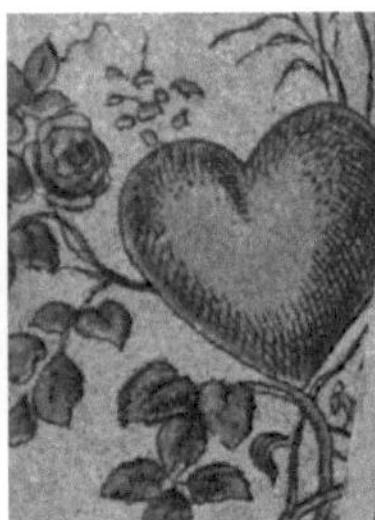 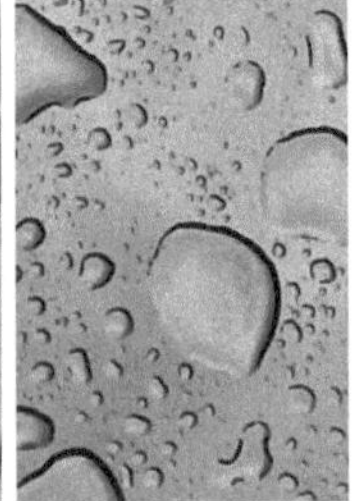 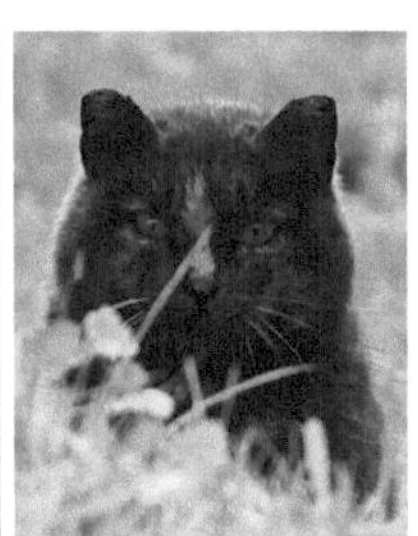

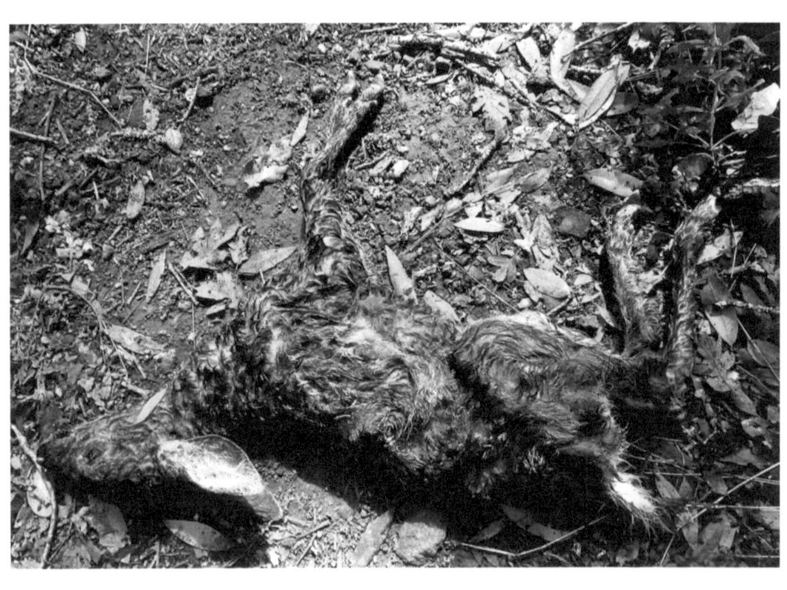

Love and Death

Simple Decoration

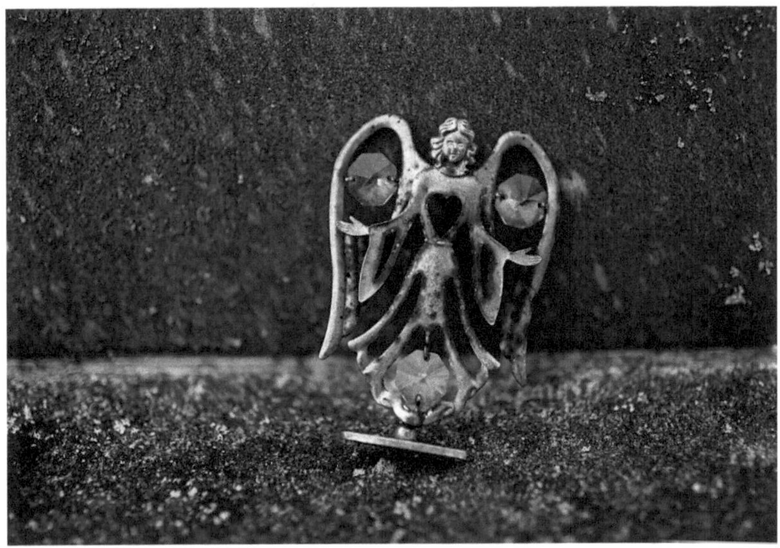

It was all Jack that Christmas.

On the drive across town I thought of nothing else, not even the weather. I ran the wipers on high, kept the defroster blasting, and concentrated on the road. My headlights carved tunnels in the slanting snow. I didn't give a thought to my ex-wife, whose car I had begged to borrow, or my daughter experiencing her first Christmas Eve without me.

My father had taught me that if I ever got caught in a blizzard to find a plow truck and follow its taillights, so on Hope Street I got behind a city plow and trailed it straight to the east side.

Jack's street hadn't been touched, but I found a clear spot in a tow zone and bumped up onto the curb. I left her there, engine running, headlights on, not caring if I saw the car again.

My key still fit, so I let myself in, stomping snow from my boots. It was late.

I was embarrassed. All the real work had been done.

Phil was there. Arthur, too. They had changed the room, repositioned the bed, set its angle, laid Jack out neat and cozy. On a pedestal table, dead center of the carpet, stood a two-foot tree, some of its branches dripping wet snow.

"The roads are treacherous," I told the room.

Someone coughed. Arthur, I think.

He was huddled by the bed, holding Jack's hand as though it were a tiny bird. It was evident he'd been crying. I shuddered a breath, believing I was too late.

Phil was behind him, sipping from a mug with my name on it. He was as even-tempered as Arthur was high-strung. From Phil's eyes I discerned that we weren't quite there yet.

"So what's the word?" I said. "What do they say?"

I reached under my scarf and fingered the collar of my coat.

"They? They don't know anything," Arthur said.

Phil rocked forward and shrugged. "Tonight. Tomorrow." He kept his eyes down. "Who knows?"

"I do. I know," Arthur said. "He'll die in the morning. He'll die on the day Christ was born."

My nerves burned cold as I approached the bed. Someone, probably Arthur, had stacked Jack's prescription bottles into a useless pyramid. I had to tuck my elbow to avoid knocking them over. No one said anything as I kissed Jack on the forehead and slowly backed away.

"That's new," I said, nodding at the tree.

"Fifteen minutes old," said Phil, tilting his watch to catch the light.

"Phil stole it from the side yard." Arthur said.

"Roots and all," Phil said.

I started to smile, then thought better of it. I leaned my face into the tree. I touched a pine needle with my nose.

"Tell me," I said. "Either one of you uncomfortable with my being here?"

Phil shrugged. "You have a right," he said. "I guess."

He was staring at Arthur, at Arthur's back.

"I don't care," Arthur said. He was studying Jack's hand as though something were written there. "Though I used to. I used to care very much. Enough to hate you both." He turned his head a little; his eyes were closed. "I suppose none of that makes a bit of difference now."

I shrugged out of my coat.

"Let me help you with that," Phil said.

It was in a hallway closet, a closet meant for coats, that we found the wicker basket full of garland and tinted-glass ornaments, and some embroidered things Jack's mother had made.

Hers was a story we'd forgotten to remember.

She'd been dead almost forever, but in her last days had crocheted tiny stockings, little candy canes, macramé angels, a few fat-faced Santas with cotton balls strategically placed.

Fine needlework!

All with a loop of yarn so you didn't need hooks. Just snatch up a branch and slip the thing on, easy as a ring.

Like fools we used it all.

We emptied that basket, crowding everything in, overlapping when we had to.

Then we settled back, sipping cocoa and admiring our handiwork.

The air grew hot with our breathing and the thick smell of pine.

I sunk into a fat chair, closed my eyes and fell asleep—for a minute or an hour.

When I woke the windows were full of light, and the tree looked gaudy and cheap—far too flashy for our friend who hated glitz.

I made my complaint out loud. And first Phil, then Arthur, agreed.

And with fresh cups of cocoa in one hand we stripped that tree bare, except for the garland and a single yellowed angel whose yarn had snarled.

God, we were tired. Each of us needed a shave. The three of us yawned like lions as we circled that tree, planning to start again, to keep it dignified and simple.

But then Jack fluttered an eye, turned his head on the pillow:

"Perfect," he whispered.

So we left it that way. ■

Cryptogram

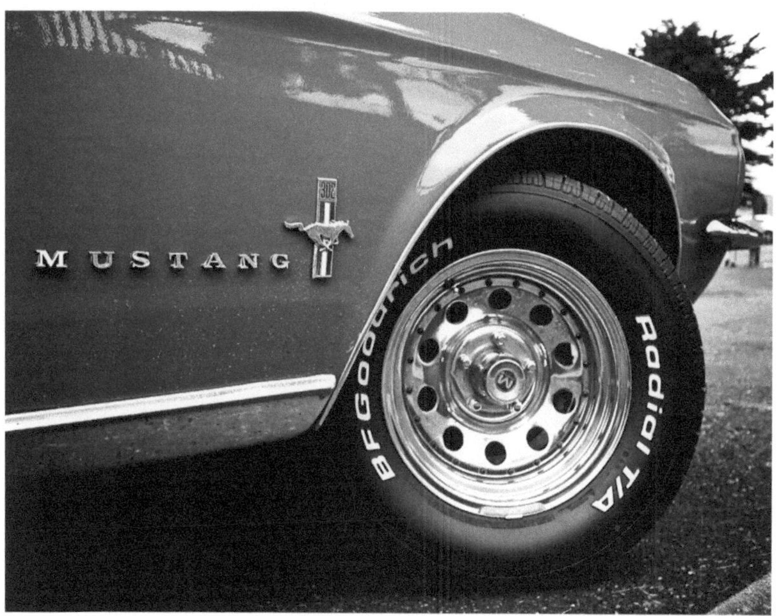

FOR WEEKS HE HACKED SO HARD WE COULDN'T UNDERSTAND much of what he was saying. His cough had worsened in a small amount of time. Between words he would launch into spasms, unleashing this deep, annoying, machine gun rattle—sort of like the jittery backfire of the souped-up '67 Mustang convertible he once stripped to its bare bones then rebuilt like a Level One "no glue necessary" snap-assembly model. The thing I remember about that car was it sitting in the driveway all the time with the hood up and him under it. No matter how many points and plugs he put into her, the timing would slip. That Ford engine wouldn't hold a tune. We couldn't drive to Stop n' Shop and back without the engine popping and banging and half the time crapping out. I was eight or nine the summer we owned it, half a lifetime ago, but I remembered the fights, the all night screaming matches over the cost of that car.

When they admitted him straight into intensive care we all believed he was on his last leg. Two doctors confirmed it. They shoved in a couple of tubes, cranked up his morphine, handed mom a bunch of double talk. I felt for the man—the sheer embarrassment of it all. After a couple of visits I started wishing he'd just hurry up and go.

Then we each got the same idea, all about the same time. I brought him a stenographer's pad and a pencil. Sissy brought him a scuba diver's chalkboard with a grease pencil on a string. And mom, the charge card queen, she went all out—she used her American Express to get him a Toshiba laptop so he could tap out whatever the hell he was trying to say.

Anyone with half a brain could see he liked the laptop best, but apparently he didn't want to offend any of us for a change, so depending on who was in the room he'd use their gift to communicate. If it was mom he'd angle the laptop so she could see the screen. In no time he had learned how to stylize the text so neither of them had to wear their glasses. For Sissy he'd scribble a big word or two on the tiny board (sometimes making a screeching sound that sent shivers up your spine). He'd write HI and BYE and OK, or if he was feeling up to it HELLO and GOOD-BYE and BETTER. Once he wrote FAREWELL, which was a rotten stunt to pull, and on Sissy of all people, because she could never take his formality in any proportion.

Possibly he sensed her resentment at being invited back to watch him . . . expire. She was eighteen, divorced, living with a drummer, and noticeably pregnant, but I swear he did it because she had cut her hair.

On my nights, Tuesdays and Thursdays, (and Sundays, if I had nothing better to do) we'd pass the pad between us. He'd jot down short sentences, hand them over; I'd make a reply and hand it back. Sometimes we played hangman or tick-tack-toe. He didn't tell me anything new, which was no surprise because he'd never said anything that I could relate to or rely on. At least nothing that didn't have something in essence to do with a combustion engine.

I thought of inquiring. I had my questions. I was sixteen, awkward and shy, afraid any day I'd have that nervous breakdown I sensed crawling around behind my eyes. But I knew how to formulate a question. Over the years I'd stored up a head full. But in the end I spared him those inquiries—despite my curiosity; no way was I going to be accused of interrogating a dying man. All total, there were eighty sheets on that pad. In our time together we filled up maybe twelve of them. And I wrote pretty big.

As it turned out the laptop blew the pad and chalkboard ideas away. Once the morphine started playing havoc with his nervous system neither Sissy nor I could make out a single letter anyway. His Gs looked like Ss, and the Ts could have been Js or Xs or anything, really. Eventually all his words started running into one another and everything he wrote appeared like a cryptogram. Mostly I just held his hand, which was an uncomfortable way to spend an evening.

If it wasn't for the Toshiba none of us would have known his last request, which was that his ashes be tossed into the wind from a lighthouse on the northern tip of Block Island. I don't know what significance that had for the two of them or even if it had anything to do with her, but to make his presence known Mom brought along the laptop. We each took turns throwing a handful of his powdery remains from the railing, and when the last of him was gone she read us this:

> WARNING: Quitting Smoking Now Greatly Reduces
> Serious Risks to Your Health. All My Love, Forever, Dad.

Which must have been his idea of a joke, really, because none of us had ever touched a cigarette, let alone smoked one, unless of course you count the secondhand smoke we were required to breathe all the years we'd told him he was killing himself. He'd quit for a short time, the summer he owned the mustang. He started right up again the day after he sold her. I thought about the significance of that on the ferry ride home, beneath a cold and brittle sun, while the wind whipped Sissy's hair, and mom, bundled up like an Eskimo, leaned dangerously over the rail, ready to drop the Toshiba like an anchor. ■

Crackers

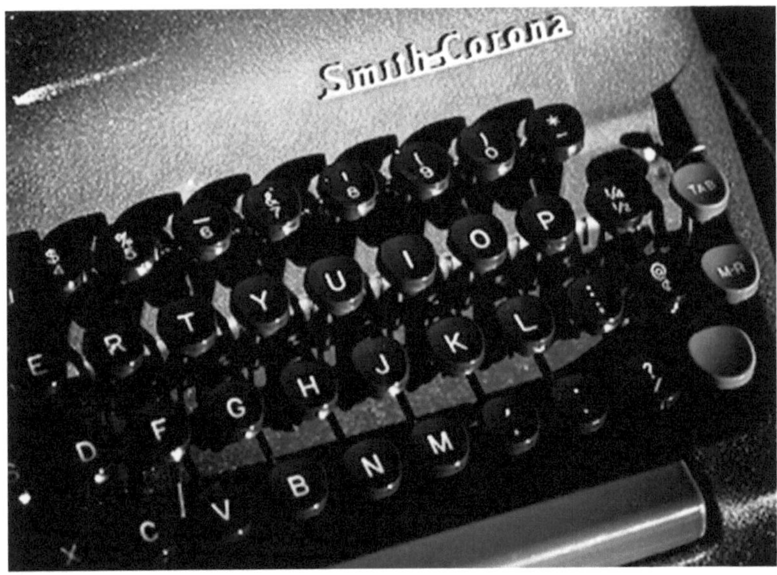

THE ROOMING HOUSE HAD A MAIN DOOR AT STREET LEVEL that was supposed to remain locked at all times but seldom was, and occasionally, especially in summer, when another roomer would wedge the door wide open with a brick, hoping to pull in some air, someone would just wander in off the street. I lived on the third floor at the far end of the long hall, the very last place on any wandering stranger's trek, so I was never bothered by these invasions, but one hot August night, while I was eating stale crackers and reading at two A.M. with my own door open, I was visited by a strange white-haired man in a rumpled sports jacket who claimed that he was from the future, my future, that he was in fact me. I didn't feel threatened. He was old and obviously unhinged, a fact made quite evident by his manner and expression: not only his mouth, but his whole face, including his tired eyes, were fixed in a deranged smile. He noticed my typewriter, and before I could rise from my chair he went over and stood beside my desk. He put one hand on the keys, and without looking aligned his fingers with the JKL;.

I expected him to start typing. Instead, with his back to me, he said, "Whatever you accomplish will be insignificant, you know, but it is vital that you never stop, never quit, not for a day, and that you don't dwell long and repeatedly on the insignificance of your work or your failure, and that you continue to do it anyway."

And what I found curious about that statement was that I had not told the man I was a writer or anything else about myself. I had barely said a word.

"Do you understand what I'm telling you?" he said.

And I nodded, though he could not see me.

"Good," he said. "I'll be on my way now."

And then, with his hand still touching the keys, he collapsed to the floor. Heart attack, the EMT said after they had lifted the old fool onto a stretcher, covered him with a sheet, and strapped him in. A policeman had come up with them. He asked me if I knew the deceased. I was still shaking, feeling I might be implicated in some sort of foul play. "No," I said, then nervously explained about the downstairs door, how the old guy had just wandered in.

"So you never saw him before?"

"No sir."

"Well, he's got no ID. Nothing in his pockets."

The officer glanced around the room, looking for I don't know what, perhaps some evidence that I was lying. Which, all these years later, as I climb the wooden steps of this old rooming house on this hot, airless night, I realize I most certainly was. ■

Mister Fumble Bumble and the Merry Widow of the Shoemaker

Every Sunday at midnight, when Death needed a new pair of shoes, he went to visit Mister Fumble Bumble, who was not himself a shoemaker though he was married to the widow of one. By luck and pure circumstance, Fumble Bumble, who was a writer and a sometimes poet, had met, seduced, then married the shoemaker's widow without any idea of the benefits of such a union. In Death's opinion, Fumble Bumble had no right to a commission on the weekly sale of shoes produced by someone else. But after wedding the shoemaker's widow, Fumble Bumble had taken complete charge of his wife's affairs, including these midnight Sunday meetings with

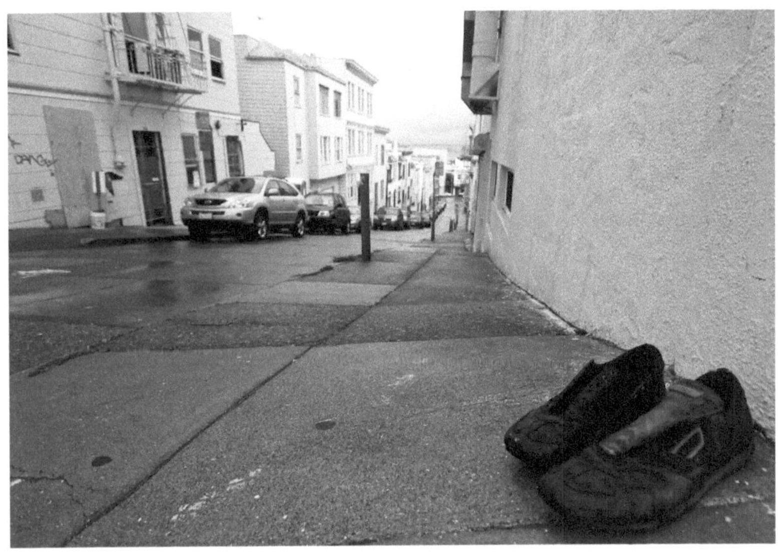

Death, during which Fumble Bumble would routinely enjoy a plate of fried food, very often chicken. No matter what was on his plate, he always offered a bit to Death, who routinely shook his head at the offer. Death didn't really mind having to sit and watch Fumble Bumble eat, though he disliked having to make dull conversation, and he deeply resented the inflated price of new shoes. Overall, he considered the slack and sloppy man sitting across from him somewhat of a pest, something between a propitious entrepreneur and a hoodwinking charlatan.

On this particular Sunday, being in a bigger hurry than usual—there were at least eight active wars in the world—Death unleashed a short rant, telling Fumble Bumble exactly what he thought of him. "You're like a little, trembling bird that just hit a window. You go in circles, flapping your wings on the ground, wavering between being a brainless buffoon and a lucky fool."

"I'm neither of those things. I'm a writer," Fumble Bumble said. "Some of my stories have won prizes. I published a book last year."

"Focus on what I'm telling you," Death said. "I'm talking to you as a friend, not a customer. We're not discussing your profession, man. Nor your personality. I'm referring to your nature, your spirit, your true underlying character, which no living creature has ever had the power to change."

Fumble Bumble frowned and lifted a drumstick to his mouth.

"I know what I'm talking about here," Death said.

"Life is flux. Living brings about change," Fumble said with a mouthful. "Our experiences shape us. They define us. Every minute of every day."

"Does it," Death said, grinning now as only Death could grin. "Or is that merely part of the wait, how one kills time pending my arrival?"

For a while neither spoke. Fumble Bumble, noticeably flustered, ate slower than usual, while Death watched him nibble and chew.

"You know, there's a distinct difference," Death explained, after he realized he had insulted Fumble Bumble. "Between a buffoon and a fool, I mean. There are advantages to each, of course, though being one thing is less tragic and less painful than being the other. You really only need to enunciate each word for your tongue to feel the ache. Say them repeatedly and follow the burning until—"

But Fumble Bumble was no longer listening. Already his head was turned, his oily lips catching the light, his mouth breaking into a polished grin at the sight of his wife, her hair loose and flowing wildly across her white silk robe, looking much like she had on their wedding night. She walked slowly, taking small deliberate steps, presenting a tray on which sat Death's shiny new shoes.

"Will these do," she said.

"Ah, you're an angel," Death said, rising from his chair.

And it was only then, caught in the blistering crossfire of their passionate stares, that Fumble Bumble realized that his wife and Death were lovers, that there never had been a shoemaker and there was no existing inventory of shoes because everyone but a fool knows death stitches together his own footwear week after week using the beautiful skins he carves from freshly broken hearts. ■

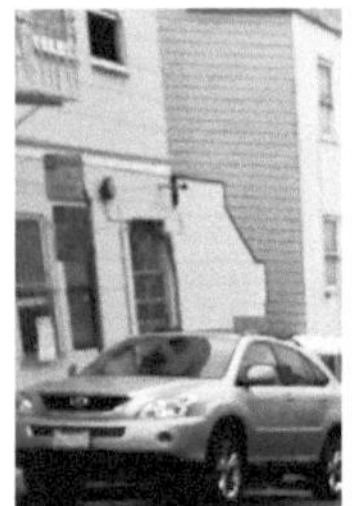
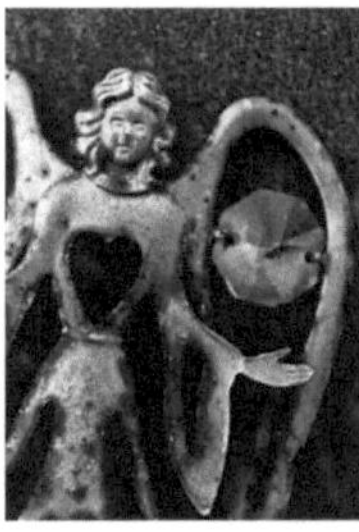
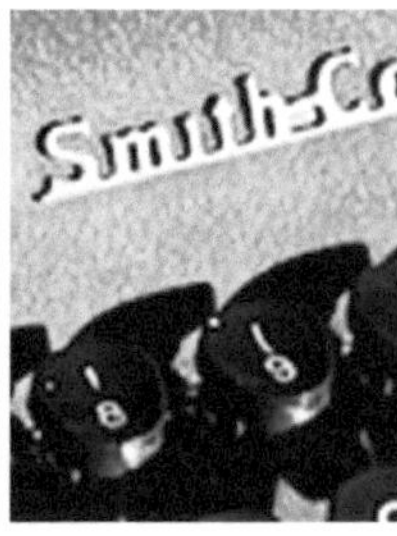
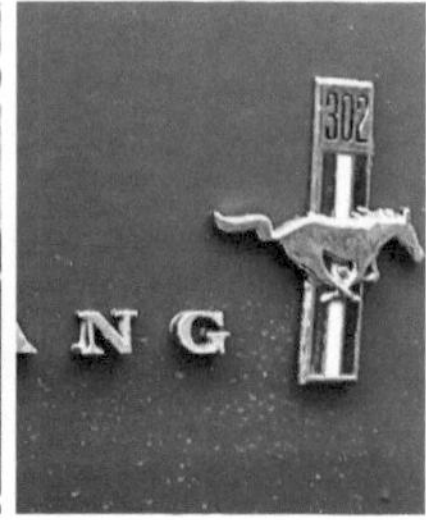

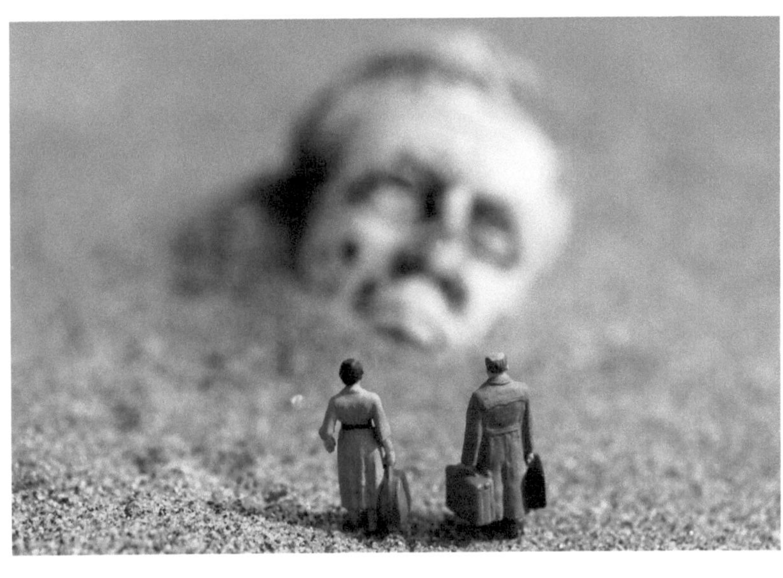

Marriage and Divorce

Mismatch

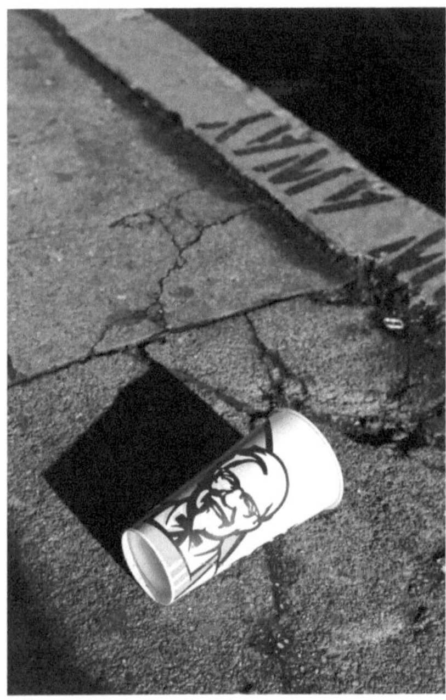

IT'S AN AUGUST NIGHT, airless and hot. The AC is on the blink. I'm in charge, so I'm working the drive-thru, leaning my head out, trying to catch a breeze, but there's nothing, no air inside or out.

I hear the bastards before I see them. I hear the engine roaring and the laughter. Four kids in a convertible, the driver racing his engine by the menu board. They start screaming all at once into the speaker box. They name combos and specials and a ton of drinks. They order a number of items not even on the menu. Then they speed past, tires screeching, exhaust pipes firing. I get a glimpse of the driver, a kid I fired a month ago. I write down the plate number, but rather than fill out an incident report, I drop my paper hat on the counter and flip the keys to a pimply girl working fries.

"Lock it up when you leave, honey." And I walk the half mile home.

Twenty minutes later I'm gnawing an ink-stained cuticle that smells like pickle juice. I've got the phone pulled out of its jack and both my lamps off. I'm fired for sure, but I don't care. I've got alimony and child support. I'm staring at the screen of my computer, trying to be a writer. Every day I practice. But today, instead of plots and characters and scenic descriptions, I'm thinking about trudging down the hall and washing my filthy over-my-ears hair. I worked noon to closing two nights in a row and a double shift today, and I haven't showered since the weekend. My clothes and my sheets and most of the furniture smell of fried food, an odor I personally can tolerate, but which the room has commandeered to entice flies and various other insects through the finger holes and gashes in the window screen.

Drawn by the glow, several flutter and land on the screen. One by one I squash them with my thumb. I'm swinging a rolled up issue of Penthouse, battling a moth the size of a humming bird when someone knocks at my door.

It's such a deceptive knock that at first I think it's the door across the hall, or one further down. "Who's that?"

"Kelly."

I move up close to the door and stare at the wood like I've got x-ray vision. I try to remember the landlady's first name, which she scribbles on her weekly receipts and which I'm sure starts with a P.

"Kelly who?"

"We haven't met. I'm new, from upstairs."

I crack the door a full two inches, and play a five second game of one-eyed peek-a-boo. It's a girl. A young woman, slouched slightly left, supporting a see-through basket of folded laundry on her modest hip. She has Wilma Flintstone hair, a pretty face, and Barbie-doll boobs.

"Hi. I'm Kelly. I just moved in." She eyes the ceiling. "Right upstairs."

I swing the door open just enough to fit my shoulders through.

I look at her face. I look at her blouse. She's under the light and I get a good long bare-bulb look at the tiny freckles parading into her shadowy cleavage.

"I hope I'm not interrupting."

"Not at all. Not at all." I swing the door open. "Would you like to come in?"

Her smile vanishes like a candle in a gale.

"Oh. What's that smell? Are you cooking something?"

My own smile, inherently crooked, pinches at my neck.

She bobs on tip toe, leaning left, then right, looking over my shoulders. "Anyway." She clears her throat, pulls a rumpled brown and yellow argyle sock from her side of the basket. "I found this. In the dryer. I thought it might be yours."

I hold my breath as I pretend to examine the object she's holding like a dead mouse.

Her nostrils twitch.

"Nope. Not mine."

Her eyes are the blue of broiler flame. She slants a look, drops the sock onto her basket. "I'm sorry. Really." And she turns, spins away, the basket high, her back arched, moving like she's got a motorized gear for a hip.

Hours later, hard rain slanting in, I wake in a sweat, clutching the argyle's mate, thrashing at the covers, dreaming I'm drowning in a sea of missing laundry. ■

Long White Banner

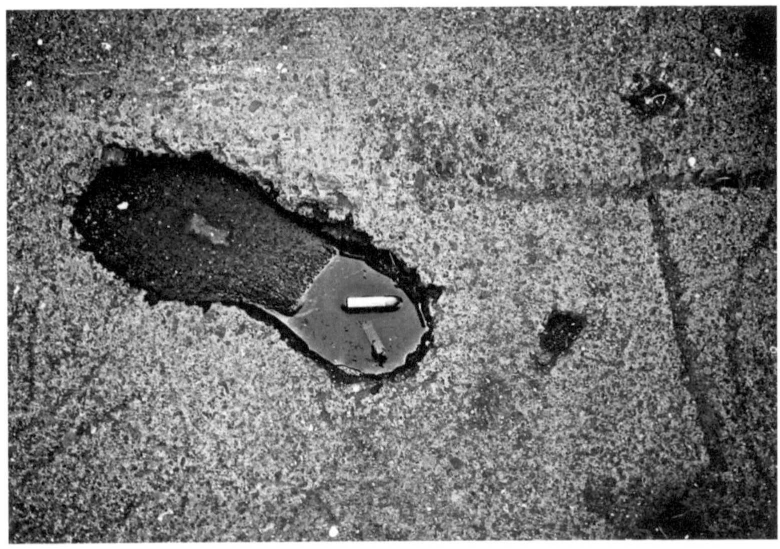

THOUGH THIS STORY IS SLIGHTLY OLDER THAN I AM, theoretically I'm in it, smack damn at its center. Nevertheless, it's not my story. If it belongs to anyone, that person would be my father, though my mother appears here, too, and she's really the person to keep your eye on. As far as I know my father has never spoken of these events aloud to anyone else. And I cannot imagine that he ever wrote them down before or after he told me. When and where he shared this story isn't nearly as important as why, but I will admit I was newly pregnant at the time, sitting in a booth at TGIF with my feet up, trying, literally, to drown my sorrows and wash away my cares with horribly sweet piña coladas. That's all I'm going to say, because I don't want to ruin anything, so from here on consider me absent and unaccounted for—just a specter in the margins, a shadow no bigger than your thumb—which is pretty much how I feel whenever I think about this story.

What my father said is this . . .

That night, while we slept, the winds shifted and the whole forecast changed. A storm off the coast, predicted to miss us by miles, rolled inland, dumping five fresh inches atop the crusted frozen landscape we'd been living with since Christmas. When I got up the wind was gusting like a hurricane, making the windows vibrate and hum. I was pretty confused. Our street hadn't been plowed and I couldn't make out the shape of our car. I heard Donna get up. I expected her to just pick up the phone, cancel her appointment, then go back to bed. Instead she made coffee, dressed without showering, brushed her teeth, knotted her hair into a ponytail, then helped me dig out the car. We sat inside it for five or ten minutes listening to the radio while the heater defogged the windows, then we set off without any mention of postponing the procedure.

The woman's clinic was halfway across town, roughly six miles. It was a boxy red brick building tucked into the sloped parking area behind the old Providence Auditorium. I had taken Donna there a week earlier for a consultation followed by a pre-examination. I hadn't gone in, but I was able to see through the windows, and I remember thinking: why wouldn't a place like that have shades or blinds; why have any windows at all?

Halfway up the hill Donna reminded me the entrance was one street over.

"I know that," I said. "This way's quicker."

My tires spun and whined on the packed snow but we made the steep incline. I moved us along a narrow street crowded with the forms of buried cars, then I swung a right. The road going down was just as steep and hadn't been plowed. A few overlapping tire tracks shone in the sun, and I tried to stay within them. I kept pumping the brakes, making the car jerk or slide, bumping Donna all over her seat.

I turned the wheel, directing the car toward the lot's entrance, but the tires didn't grab, and I missed the opening by three car lengths. I acted as though that was my intention and casually steered us into a vacated spot adjacent to the old auditorium. But it was low, really low, leaving an icy uphill climb.

Donna didn't wait for me to shut off the engine. She threw open her door and huffed ahead, her bag slung over her shoulder. She dug her boots into the snow, crunching her footsteps, high stepping like she was conquering Everest.

She stopped climbing the instant she saw the people with their signs. More than a dozen were huddled near the entrance, their mouths streaming vapor in the cold morning air. Most were carrying nothing more than poster-sized black and white photographs; blurred enlargements of curled fetuses. There were a couple of homemade wooden crosses with infant dolls nailed to them. Two women, both young and one of whom appeared very pregnant, held the ends of a long white banner painted with GOD KNOWS in dripping red letters.

"Relax," I said. "There must be another way in. A side entrance, maybe."

I studied the building for a moment. Small mountains of plowed snow surrounded the place, making it look like part of a Christmas village.

Donna slid her bag off one shoulder and hitched it onto the other. She was focused on the main entrance where the picketers had scrambled for position, creating a corridor for a young couple exiting the building. A chant broke out. It was just mumble jumble, a drone I couldn't understand.

Donna did an immediate about-face and started back down toward the car. She got into the passenger seat and closed the door. I stood with my back against a telephone pole and watched the picketers. They had pulled back and broken up into small groups. Some held coffee cups or cigarettes along with their signs. A few seemed engaged in conversation, but overall they looked cold and bored.

After a minute I walked down to the car and got in. Donna had a cigarette going. She held it close to her chin, her arms crossed high.

I asked if she was okay, and she shook her head no. Her cheeks hollowed as she pulled smoke. "Just take me home," she said.

I turned the key. The engine caught the first time. The heater was still warm.

"It's Saturday," I said. "We'll come back during the week." I moved a lever and directed air at our feet. "Saturday was probably a bad choice."

"Let's not talk about bad choices right now," Donna said. She streamed smoke at the windshield. "Please," she said.

I pumped the brakes and rolled us down. On our right along the gray wall of the old auditorium a line of windows had been boarded with squares of plywood. At the corner Donna cranked down her window a couple of inches and tossed her cigarette into the snow.

"These people must have jobs," I said, and made the turn. "They can't be here all the time."

Donna tilted her head against her door. She left it there as I swayed us into the left lane, pointing us home. Behind us a car honked. The light was red. I put my hand on Donna's leg and gave it a firm squeeze. Tears ran out of her eyes and over the bridge of her nose.

"We'll call and reschedule," I said. "For a weekday. Saturday was a bad idea. We'll call the minute we get home."

Donna nodded. Her eyes were closed, but it was a definite nod, which I took as a bona fide sign of agreement. We had a pact. No kids until I was done with college and in a good paying position. I'd work hard, put in extra hours, get us a nice house, then we could begin to think seriously about children.

The landlord was supposed to shovel after a storm, but our walkway hadn't been touched, and Donna didn't appear very steady, so without asking I looped an arm around her waist and scooped her up. She didn't resist but she didn't help either. Rather than loop her arms around my neck and hold on, she just slumped against my chest, a dead weight. Twice I lost my balance, dipped, and nearly fell, but each time I miraculously regained my footing by more or less stumbling forward. When we got to the stoop, I set Donna down on the first step. She climbed to the top stair, but before she opened the door, she gave me a look—a fleeting, pinched stare that burned right through me. It reminded me of the look my mother would give whenever she caught me eating out of the sugar bowl.

Once inside, I turned up the heat then began to brew fresh coffee. Donna headed straight to the bedroom and threw herself face first onto the bed without taking her coat off.

She never called the clinic to reschedule. We barely exchanged another word on the subject, except for one long, ugly argument, right after I had dropped my courses and taken a job as an assistant manager at Burger King. Other than that one fiasco, we remained civil to one another, and whenever someone mentioned the A-word we quickly changed the topic. Same with the TV. If we heard the subject mentioned, one of us lounged for the set. You had to change the channel by hand in those days. No remotes. No cable. A lot less stations, fewer choices. The three major networks gave you your news at noon and at six, then again at eleven. The rest of the time you just settled for what they gave you and tried to make the best of it. ■

Door Prize

When Carol told me the Miller place was in foreclosure, I felt we'd been swindled. The Millers owned the largest, most luxurious home on our street and the only one Carol and I had never set foot inside. Eighteen times in three years Jordan and Martin Miller had shared dinner in our home or attended a summer barbecue in our backyard. Eighteen meals without a single reciprocal invitation. We weren't exactly friends, but we were good neighbors, and that lopsided score seemed impossible to explain. We lived just five houses away, in a two-bedroom cottage on the curve of the cul-de-sac.

Jordan had been a no-show at Carol's baby shower. Then, around the time our daughter was born, Martin had gone missing. Rumor was he had caught

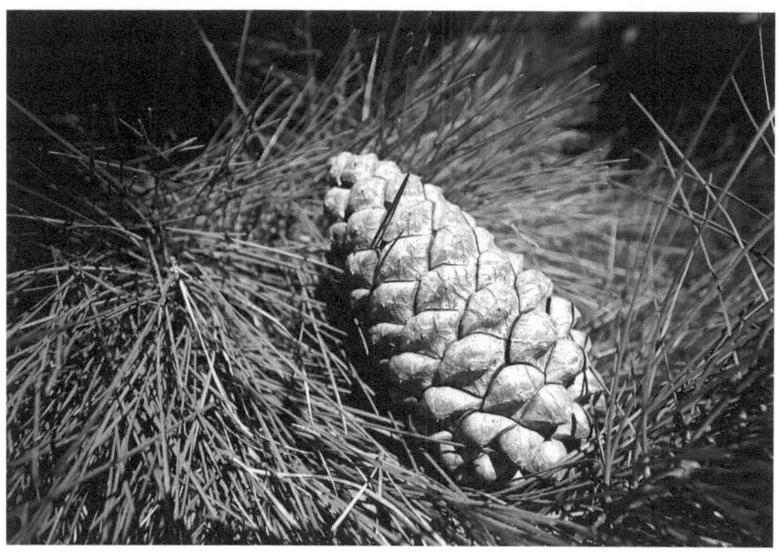

his wife red-handed at something far too perverse to speak about. Details were lacking, but a judge had granted him sole custody of his teenage boy. Martin moved the kid to another town and promptly filed for bankruptcy.

How much of this was reliable, I didn't know. Jordan kept a low profile. Her car was never in the driveway, and their lawn looked like shit. The house appeared vacant.

Then one Saturday, Carol and I saw her across two checkout lanes at the Super Stop n' Shop. I didn't recognize her. She had dyed her hair stark white. It was chopped shorter than ever and looked slightly ridiculous with her unseasonable tan.

"Check out the ping-pong ball earrings on Miss Tubby," Carol said.

Jordan blew a kiss across the lanes. Carol blew one back.

"Pinch me so I don't laugh," Carol said.

I waved and waved.

The woman had grown heavy, but she still had a lot of curves.

The following morning, an invitation, handwritten and without postage, was mixed with our mail.

Dear Carol & Bill,
Please Attend My "Farewell and Sayonara" Party,
Friday @ Seven. Food, Drinks & Door Prizes.
Love & kisses,
Your future Ex-Neighbor, JM

"What do you think?" I said. "Wanna go?"

Carol arched her eyebrows. "Absolutely. That bleached blonde cow still owes me a baby gift."

Friday night, Carol said, "Guess her measurements. Win the door prize."

We stood beneath an archway of inlaid marble in a vestibule as big as our dining room. Jordan was nowhere in sight, and none of the guests had noticed us yet.

The living room was enormous. A stairway curved upward on both sides. Looped between the high posts a wide banner with foil lettering read GOOD LUCK JORDAN!

"Buy me this house," Carol said.

"Sure thing," I said, "Can you wait until I get my coat off?"

"A coat was a bad idea," Carol said.

I twisted out of the sleeves. "Who knew we'd be driving over."

"Just remember to pick up milk and Pampers when you take Larissa home."

Larissa was our babysitter.

"Not my turn," I said. "I drove her last time."

Carol moved ahead of me, stepping down into plush cream carpet. She stood poised on one foot, presenting herself to the room.

"Is that Carol," someone shouted from a corner.

Carol did a half curtsey, then a complete ballerina turn.

There were two simultaneous wolf whistles.

"Oh look, it's the Carsons," said a voice thick with booze.

"Not the crazy Carsons," someone chimed in.

I scanned the room, clutching my coat. I didn't see a single person I wanted to talk to. And to make matters worse there wasn't a coat rack or a closet anywhere in sight.

Jordan bumped through the crowd and started towards us—I hoped to rescue my coat.

"Hallelujah, thank you Christ," she cried, "At last, someone to dance with."

She took several rapid baby steps, teetering on thin heels—a drink in one hand, a cigarette in the other. Carol performed another sweeping curtsey; on the half-turn she exaggerated a wink in my direction.

"Careful cowboy, " she hissed. "Here comes the stampede."

"No secrets you two," Jordan said and laughed a high laugh.

The closer she got the more her dress rippled with light.

Carol murmured through a crooked mouth, "Who does she think she's fooling with that outfit?"

I said, "Jordan, you look fantastic!"

To Carol I whispered, "Behave yourself for one drink."

"Wanna bet she can crack walnuts with those thighs," Carol said.

The rest is embarrassing to admit. After four martinis and two fast dances, I fucked our gracious host against a stockade fence—a quick frantic unsatisfying fuck behind the pool shed with a heavy branch of pine needles scratching at my face. After which, without a word between us, we returned to the party.

"Hey! Who wants to see my high school yearbook?" Jordan said.

Of course I didn't. I just wanted to get out of there.

I found Carol in the hall, sipping champagne, and wearing my coat like a cape.

"Who'd you get in a cat fight with?" she said.

Blood was oozing from the scratches on my face. I told her a story, a hastily made up tale. The mind is incredible under pressure. A mere one hundred feet from the scene of the crime, I convinced my wife to feel sorry for me.

She fingered beneath the wound, called me poor baby, then walked me out into the cool evening air. She drove us home, delivered the babysitter across town, brought back milk and Pampers, then came to bed with a lighted candle and a small round tin of pink gel.

"What's that?"

"Salve for those scratches," she said. "Sit up."

Her hair was wild. The candle lit up her eyes as she smeared a gob of ointment over my wound. She spread it thick. The pungent odor tickled my nostrils. I used to be a boy scout and once worked as a caterer's assistant, so I know the smell of Sterno, but it was too late.

"Close your eyes," Carol said, tilting the candle closer. "This is definitely going to sting." ■

Old Sharp Photo

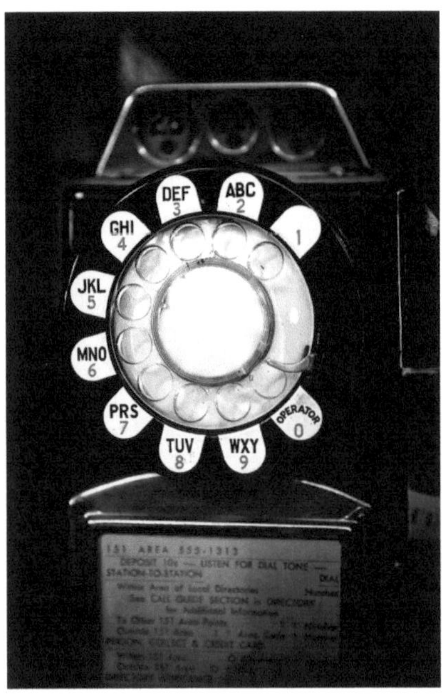

It's crazy you even recognize her voice, creepy that she's somehow tracked you down after all these years, downright silly that you're standing in socks, stained briefs, a yellowed t-shirt with a cigarette burn beside your navel (put there purposely one night, just to see if you could still feel), but what makes it all feel like some bizarre lost episode of the Twilight Zone is the phone isn't even your phone. It's not in your name, not your number, just a privately owned, coin-fed payphone mounted on a wall of a dilapidated rooming house for men only, and as far as you know the number is private, unlisted, not in any directory in the world, printed or otherwise. So how in hell . . . ?

You hate this phone more than you have hated any phone before. Once a week, usually Saturday morning, the superintendent uses a stubby little key to open the coin box, and every time you catch him emptying it, you open your door a crack, make some small talk, then plead with him to turn the ringer volume down, and each time he gives you the same hard look, then says the same thing: he doesn't know how, he has no idea how to regulate the volume, and he reminds you he's told you that like a million times, then he invites you to take a look, so again you look and you see nothing—no lever, no knob, no adjustment mechanism. You can't do anything, he can't do anything, so nothing changes, and you get stuck answering the thing day and night to stop the shrill ringing, though you rarely use the phone to make calls yourself, despite the convenience of it being mounted three steps outside your door, a location that creates hallway gridlock, especially on weekend nights. The thing's a fucking nuisance, totally useless to you because you've never once given the number to anyone. Who in hell would you give it to?

But here you are answering again, late on a Sunday night, hearing your ex-wife's voice, recognizing the deep, flinty, suggestive tone, understanding who's calling in a heartbeat. She says, hey, how you doing, like the two of you chatted yesterday, not ten years ago, then she doesn't wait for a response, so you figure okay she's high or drunk or demented, because it's been ten years. She says, listen, yesterday I was cleaning out a closet and found a box full of useless junk and at the bottom of the box was a picture, a snapshot, a black and white, no frame, just an eight by ten glossy with the two of us in our pajamas sitting across from each other eating breakfast, though I suppose it could be lunch or dinner, you can't see what's on our plates, but it's a really nice shot, tightly focused, very sharp, plenty of natural light, probably because in those days we never hung curtains, we couldn't afford curtains, remember, so you can see our faces, half our faces, good and sharp like a couple of statues in perfect profile, excellent detail, as I say black and white but with all the shades of gray, and we look so young and pretty, goddamned happy the two of us, though in an odd pretty hard to describe way, neither of us is really smiling, in our expressions there's not a trace of worry, no stress lines, no tension, just youthful lazy calmness radiating almost serene the way our eyes are lined up, a remarkable photo but for the life of me I can't remember where it came from, who snapped it, if we were on acid or why anyone would be in our kitchen taking snapshots so early, I'm assuming it's morning, so why would anyone especially a skilled photographer with obvious talent, so what I'm guessing is it was taken right before we got married the summer when all your artsy pals and their hippy girlfriends used to wander in, crash on the couch, pass out on the carpet, make themselves at home eating whatever they could find after we had gone to bed after telling them all to please keep the stereo and all conversation down to a dull roar because our neighbors had real lives and the landlady's son was a cop, remember, so we implored them to cool it with the volume on the music, and shut off the lights, lock the door when they left, which any of them rarely did, but most importantly extinguish all candles, incense sticks, joints, cigarettes, pipes, remember that fat piano player Peter who always smoked cherry tobacco in a corncob pipe and once snorted heroin then burned a huge hole in the couch, you made him swear to leave nothing burning ever fearing next time the whole house would go up in flames while we slept, dreaming our future, believing we were moving even in sleep toward some magical idyllic life we'd share together, though that didn't exactly happen now did it, she said, coughing, laughing, her voice trailing off not with a question mark but a verbal exclamation point that drops into a silence that stretches out until it actually makes the phone vibrate before you suspect she has hung up, leaving you there with the cord tangled under one arm, looped once around your waist, pacing the tight space the cord allows, holding the phone a full minute before you understand the silence isn't attached to her, not a pause while she lights another cigarette, not her brooding, but a terminated connection. The line is dead and it's a done deal, which, considering you haven't spoken a single word, is equivalent to picking up the phone as you so often will, half-asleep and dull-headed, picking up just to stop the ringing, frequently hearing the voice of some stranger, usually a man looking for a man, but sometimes a woman sighing across the wire in exasperated breathless fashion, declaring she's sorry, so terribly sorry, she's a wreck, her hand is shaking, and she's apparently misdialed the number, reached the wrong man, whoever in hell you are. ■

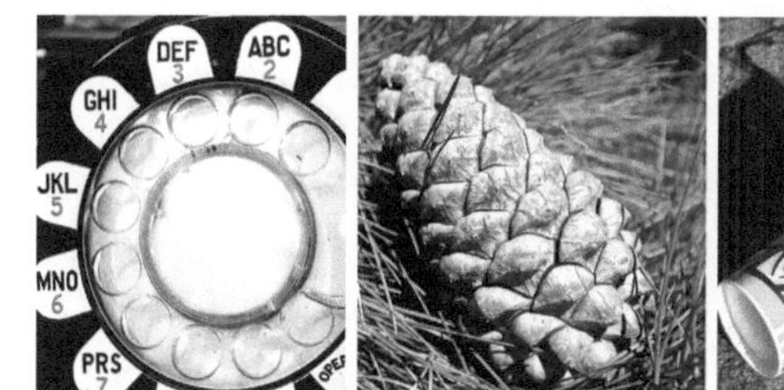
DEF
3
ABC
2
GHI
4
JKL
5
MNO
6
PRS
7
TUV
WXY
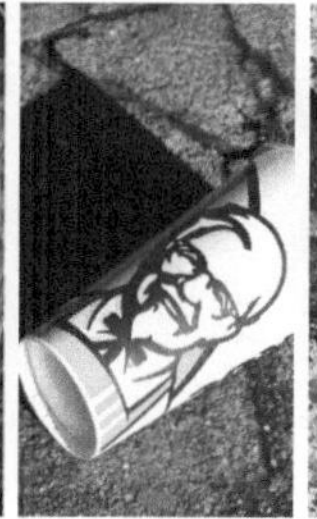
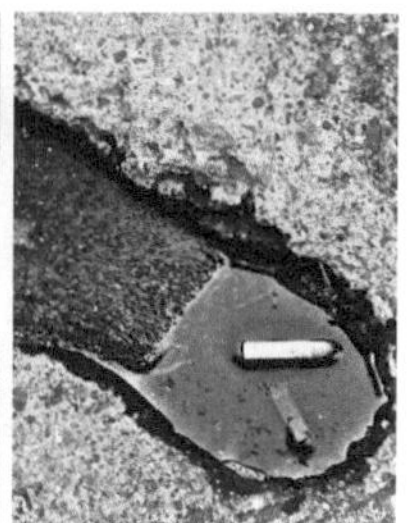

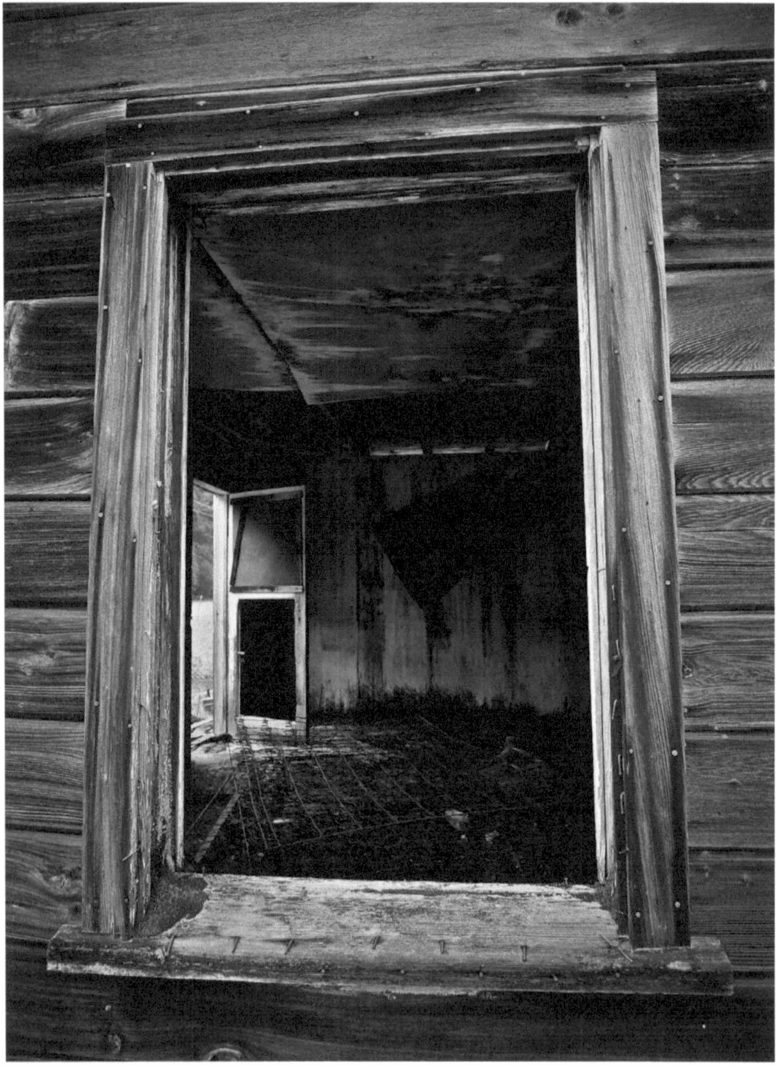

The Wicked and the Virtuous

A Woman on the Bus

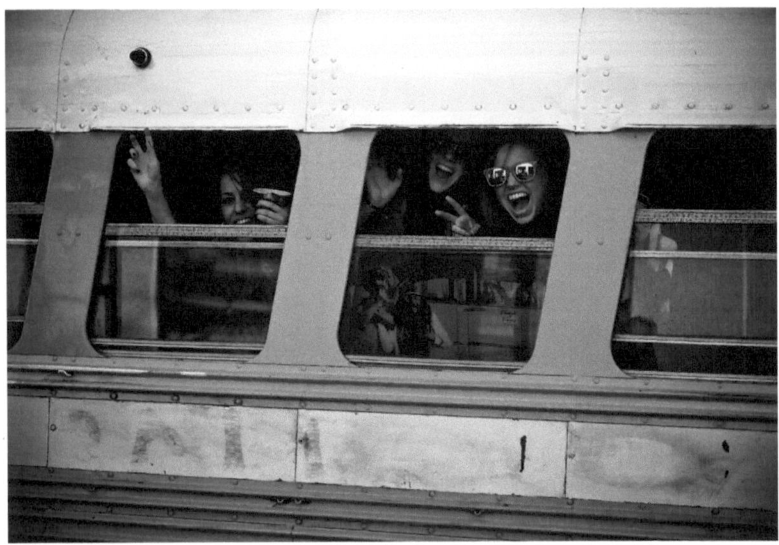

HE WAS RETURNING HOME AFTER ATTENDING A LONG WAKE and a short funeral the first time he saw her. She was all dressed in pink, head to toe—including the plastic barrettes in her hair, her frosty eye shadow, creamy lipstick, and slick fingernails. She sat directly across from him in the long seat opposite his at the front of the bus.

He made an entry of the sighting in his notebook. A woman/child made of cotton candy, he wrote.

The next time he saw her she was all dressed in blue with white plastic hoop earrings big as bracelets, and he decided she was either a couple years younger or much older than he had initially assumed.

The next time he saw her she was all dressed in pink again. Barelegged, bony kneed, a Band-Aid on her ankle, no laces in her sneakers.

The next time he saw her she wore plaid everything, except for her Buster Brown shoes. She was telling a man with a brown cap that she had released her equity, consolidated her assets, become bullish on America.

The next time he saw her she was humming holiday music. Brahms, he thought.

The next time he saw her she and the driver were chatting, both sipping from identical white Styrofoam cups that were giving off steam from whatever they held within.

The next time he saw her she asked if he could spare a sheet from his notebook, and when he gave her a blank page she tore off just a corner and handed the rest back. A moment later she asked if she could use his pen. Later he saw her give the folded scrap to the driver.

The next time he saw her she seemed jumpy, out of sorts. She kept touching her hair.

The next time he saw her she was pregnant but not by much.

The next time he saw her she was telling the bus driver that he was a good and decent man, a super nice guy, but would never be able to keep her in the way to which she had become accustomed.

The next time he saw her she just smiled. Not at him so much as everyone while she rubbed her belly like it was a magic lantern.

The next time he saw her she was no longer pregnant, which he thought rather odd.

The next time he saw her she was in obvious pain, bent forward, clutching her belly, as though pressed sore by heavy affliction.

The next time he saw her, she was quite composed.

The next time he saw her, she said, "That is the most wonderful news I have heard in a long time. Good for you. What a blessing. Congratulations." She wasn't looking at him or at anyone. Her eyes in fact were closed and he had no idea whom she was addressing.

The next time he saw her she was sitting up close to the driver, and he heard her whisper, "Because you say so. No sir, I do not think so."

The next time he saw her she said to a child sitting on a mother's lap, "You're not really a little monster are you?"

The next time he saw her, she said hello, or at least her lips formed the shape of that sound and her tongue clicked both syllables.

The next time he saw her she told him she was surprised, shocked, stunned, flabbergasted. He didn't inquire what she meant.

The next time he saw her she was with another woman, an older woman not quite old enough to have been her mother but perhaps an aunt or older sister, and they were both dressed in basic black with pillbox hats that sprouted long veils big as mosquito nets.

The next time he saw her he was sure she was dying, though quite unofficially and entirely without permission.

The next time he saw her she looked lovelier, more beautiful than ever, more so than the first sighting, which didn't seem possible, and so he decided he was merely dreaming about her. Again.

The next time he saw her she told him that she wanted to be no more than friends.

The next time he saw her she seemed completely withdrawn.

The next time he saw her she rose from her seat and signaled to the driver, and the bus moved away with its doors still open before he could catch up.

The next time he saw her she was rather aloof, and when he told her he was keeping notes, a record of sorts, then opened the notebook to read a few sentences, she told him to please shut up because she didn't feel at all like talking and the sun's glare was giving her a headache.

So he moved to a seat further back and shut his eyes, which took a great deal of effort, one that required more energy than it should, so much energy that the effort to keep them closed left him drained, weak, empty.

Which led him to believe the entire affair must have been less than true love, no more than infatuation.

Which in turn led him to reflect on the very first time he had seen her, that morning after the funeral, though for the life of him he could not now remember who had passed away.

The last time he saw her she was naked against the moon, just a silhouette highlighted by gray shadow, but still, anyone could see she was a witch, a hag, an incubus in her ugliest form. And he took that as a warning. ■

Here and Here and Here

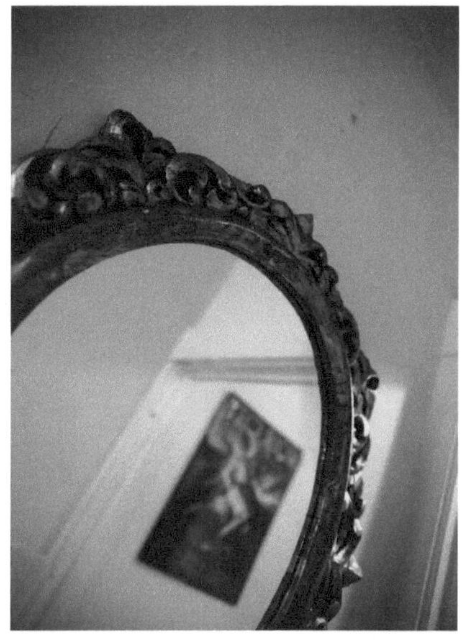

LAST TIME I SAW LARRY Baldwin was the night Sally—Larry's third wife, a retired exotic dancer less than half his age—dropped the mirror and the cocaine went flying. For the next minute and a half the shag carpet became our entire focus. Larry came around from the bar to get a better view. He brought his drink and the little razor blade on a chain that he'd used to cut the coke.

We weren't friends, Larry and I. Not really. He was an ex-neighbor, a retired Navy man the same age as my father, and he had a little money, and I think he genuinely liked me. So we gambled together, drank and ate, and snorted coke together. But beyond those things we had nothing in common and very little to talk about.

Now we stood facing one another, Larry and me, with Sally on her knees between us. She was dragging her long fake fingernails through the carpet, clawing with both hands through the deep shag.

I think I see some of it, she said. Do you see? Right here, and here, and here. Do you see it, Larry, she said.

Barely ninety seconds had passed since the drop, the accident, the calamity. I really didn't know what to call it. I was in shock. Some of the coke on the mirror, one of the long thick neat lines that Larry always took great pains to prepare, was mine. There was plenty more in a cellophane bag on the bar, but Larry was a funny kind of guy, and when someone or something swung his mood to the gloomy side then the party was over and it was time to go home. And I didn't want to go home, not yet. And for reasons which I won't go into here I didn't want this party to be over—not then. I wanted my line. I wanted nothing else. Not Larry's goodwill. Not his fake smile. Not even another more genuine smile from his sultry wife, whom later, long after Larry went to bed, clawed at my ass with her sharp nails, holding me in, making me cum inside of her, whispering, "Don't worry. It's all right, honey, it's fine, I want to make a baby, I do. My womb is a cold empty place and I need a human heart to warm it."

After she went to bed, I helped myself to another line, a long fat one. And as I snorted it up my nostrils I stared at the face of the man in the mirror looking up at me. He was smarter than me. I could tell by his eyes. He knew he should never have come here. And I knew he would never be back. ■

Entry Level

My son called me at this sports bar where I regularly help out on weekends. He had been staying with my new wife and me. But it wasn't working out. He'd just gotten out of juvey jail—a detention center over in Harrisburg. My new wife was a former nun turned floor scrubbing evangelist. Her name was Ellie. She was a good-hearted woman with no tolerance for transgression. My boy and she couldn't stand one another. I figured his phone call meant more trouble.

"Dad, I got in."

"Got in where?" I said.

I thought maybe our prayers had been answered, that he had found his own apartment or signed up for the military. He was my blood but I didn't need more of his grief. He was seventeen and handsome, a bright kid full of dirty tricks like his mother.

"Are you listening? This is entry level."

I tucked the phone under my chin. Two waitresses with high lacquered hair

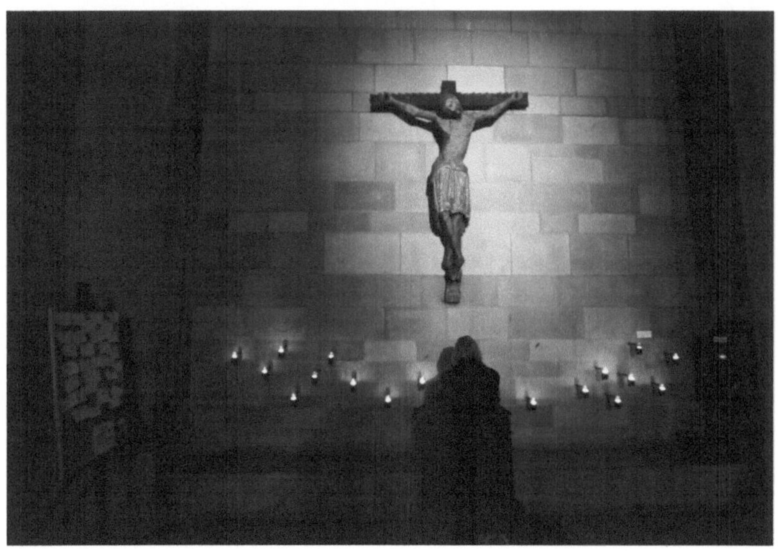

were waving drink orders. I leaned toward them but the cord wouldn't reach. I gave the one-minute finger and they frowned at each other.

"For god's sake, Carl," said one, snapping her gum. "I'm trying to make a living here."

My son was yakking about something—a new job, a new life. He sounded excited, a little too excited. I wondered if he was high, on what, and where he'd gotten the money. Lately Ellie went to bed with her purse beneath her pillow.

The waitresses were getting antsy.

"Can we talk later," I said into the phone. "The place is filling up with people from a hockey game, and I've got two fat guys waving pennants in my face."

"Who you calling fat," said one of the girls.

I got home half past two. The house was dark, quiet. When I walked past my son's room I saw Ellie jump up off the bed. She was red-faced and sweaty. Her hair was down and her robe was open.

"What were you doing," I said.

She gathered her robe around the middle and fastened the tie. She didn't say anything. She tried to move past me and I clamped a hand on her arm. She was blonde and fragile, with bones like a bird. Her pulse was racing.

"Ellie," I said.

"It's not what you think," she said, pushing past me.

I stayed in the doorway and decided I didn't know what to think.

I went over to the bed to check on my son. I leaned close and watched him breathe. He was the spitting image of me, a carbon copy. On the floor by the bed I found a pair of Ellie's panties crumpled into a ball. I plucked them up and carried them into the living room.

Ellie was on the sofa smoking a cigarette. Her hand and her jaw were trembling. A gray cloud had formed above her head.

I threw the underwear at her. "Jesus Christ," I said. "I don't know how to deal with something like this, I really don't."

"Well, I can't help you," my wife said and blew smoke across the room.

I said, "Would you mind telling me what you were planning to do in there?"

"I'm not sure," my wife said. "I didn't go in with a plan. It just happened."

"It?" I said.

"This," she said. She waved her cigarette. "All of this."

I sat down on the sofa arm. "He's seventeen," I said.

"He acts older. He looks older. He could pass for twenty-five."

She said this proudly, as if he belonged to her.

"He reminds me of you, how you were," she said, pulling smoke.

"Well he's not me," I said.

She tapped her cigarette into the big ashtray. "Listen," she said. "I don't think we should discuss this now. I know it's hard, but I think the best thing, the rational thing for us to do is wait until morning. We'll all be fresh and far more reasonable then. We'll sit down, the three of us. This is something that needs talking about," she said, getting up. "But not at half past two in the morning."

I felt like breaking her in half. I thought about it. First her, then him. I could kill them both and set the house on fire. A gallon of gasoline and a match, that's all it would take. But she was right. She was always right. Never struggle in the absence of the light. Never battle demons with sleepies in your eyes.

Always turn your face to the light and the power and keep your back to the shadows. She had taught me these things.

I cried for almost five minutes, straight sobbing, worse than a baby. Then I asked her if she wanted to pray with me. I got down on the carpet by her feet, and started without her. I started with the Lord's prayer but she put her hand on my head and she said, "Carl, please don't go crazy on me now. Please, don't. Save your prayers for tomorrow. We're all going to need them."

In this too I felt she was right.

After she went into the bedroom, I fixed a spot on the sofa. Then I got her sleeping pills from the medicine chest. I spilled four into my hand and swallowed them without water. I went into the kitchen and found the cooking sherry. I gulped a mouthful to give the pills a kick. On the way back to the couch I heard my son cough. I thought about waking him. I stood by his door for half a minute. Then I heard Ellie in the other room whispering the Lord's prayer without me.

Four pills were too many. I woke up too slowly. My head throbbed and the backs of my eyeballs ached. I couldn't arrange one thought in front of the other. Up until I checked the drawers and threw open the closets, I figured they'd both gone to church. ■

A Proper Investigation

I SUFFER FROM NIGHT BLINDNESS, SO COLLEEN DROVE. I USED my key light and studied the map the whole ride. In my mind I didn't think this meeting would prove any more eventful than the other times we had been promised reliable information. But my heart still ached. My heart ached and my stomach rumbled as Colleen directed us downtown, under bridges; she found the side-street without once consulting me.

She shut off the engine and the headlights.

I looked at the building.

"I'm not going to go in," she said.

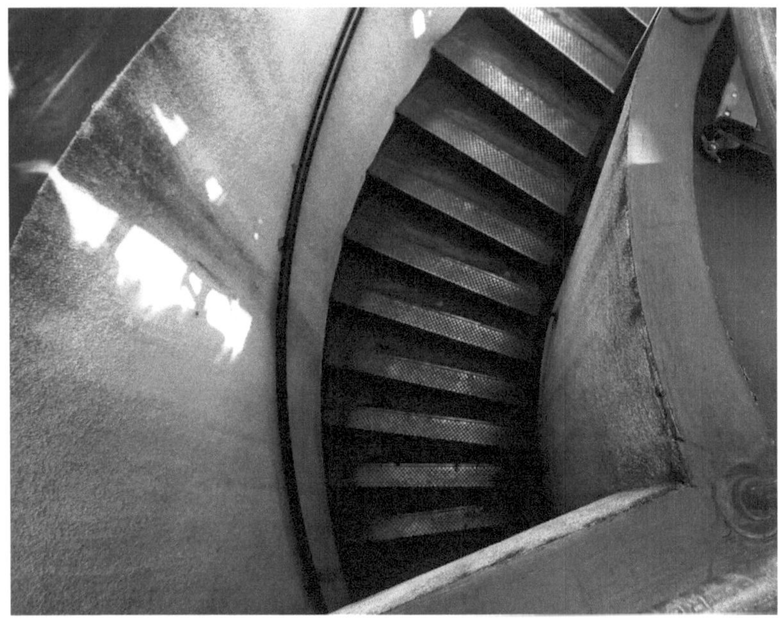

"Are you sure," I said.

"I'd only make things worse. I'll sit here and smoke," she said.

I squeezed her hand, then got out and went inside.

The lobby was empty except for a folding chair and a small pile of newspapers.

Taped to the wall at the base of the stairs was a handwritten sign on a sheet of 3-hole notebook paper. Spelled out in block letters was: Midnight Detective and Security Services. Beneath the name a penciled arrow pointed up.

I climbed one flight and found another sheet of notebook paper. Same message. The arrow pointed left.

I moved down a short hallway that smelled like old wet laundry, turned a corner, and walked into the only lighted space, then past a bare desk into a larger office.

The man looked like a kid with a penciled mustache.

The cuffs of his pinstripe suit were miles too long.

He wore a bright yellow bow tie.

At the sight of me he folded his cell phone without comment and put the device away. I was glad he made no effort to shake my hand.

"Mister Thurber?"

I nodded.

"This won't take a minute," he said.

He showed the way with a wave of his hand, like a game show host.

Near the window was a kitchen table and two vinyl backed chairs. He had arranged the photos like he was playing solitaire.

"Make yourself comfortable," he said.

I sat sideways on the furthest chair and looked at the upside-down photographs.

"You might be more comfortable sitting on this side."

"No, this is fine," I said.

I watched him set frameless bifocals on the end of his nose. He bent at the waist and leaned uncomfortably close.

"I also have copies of the motel registry and the credit card receipt. The man's an Episcopalian minister, believe it or not."

"I don't care about the man."

"Of course you don't."

I hadn't more than glanced at the photos. He looked at me looking at him, and he moved his tongue around the inside of his mouth. Then he tapped a finger on a cockeyed close up.

"That the same girl?"

I looked but I didn't need to look.

I nodded.

"Very attractive," he said.

I nodded and wondered if I should thank him and walk away, tell Colleen it's all been another mistake, another close call.

"There's more, a second roll of film, shot after this one," he said, "but it's not developed yet. I'm expecting a call on it soon."

I thought about what your life becomes if you don't keep an eye on it every minute.

"The next step, of course, is up to you."

He removed the spectacles, folded them flat.

"I can bring her to you, or bring them both to you. In any condition you want them to arrive."

I moved to his side of the table. Just two photos showed Janet's face; most were of her back or an awkward side angle, or of her behind, or of a man's hairy ass with her on her side, one leg folded beneath.

"She has her mother's long toes," I said.

He tapped a close-up of her foot.

"That one there is my oddball favorite."

He held the photo up by its corner. I turned half around.

"See how I caught the light? That tiny sparkle?"

He turned the image. Held it six inches from my face while I examined the spangle of reflected light.

"We gave her that anklet," I said.

"Excuse me?"

"That's what my wife will say. She'll say we gave her everything, anything she ever needed or wanted. But that can't be right, now can it?" ■

Loot

Once I had him down I kicked the bastard in the face and neck until he stopped moving, then I fished through the pockets of his three-piece suit, grabbed his wallet, and ran. I raced across the park until I got a pain in my side, then I walked for a while. This was ten or eleven o'clock at night, the moon glowing like a street lamp. I sat on a bench shadowed by evergreens, caught my breath, and looked around. I saw a lady walking her dog, a small white puffy poodle pulling at the leash so that it looked like a mop on a stick. Nobody noticed me sitting there so I took out the wallet. No cash, no credit cards. Just a driver's license, a few business cards, and a photo of a pretty red-haired woman wearing too much lipstick. I lit a cigarette and

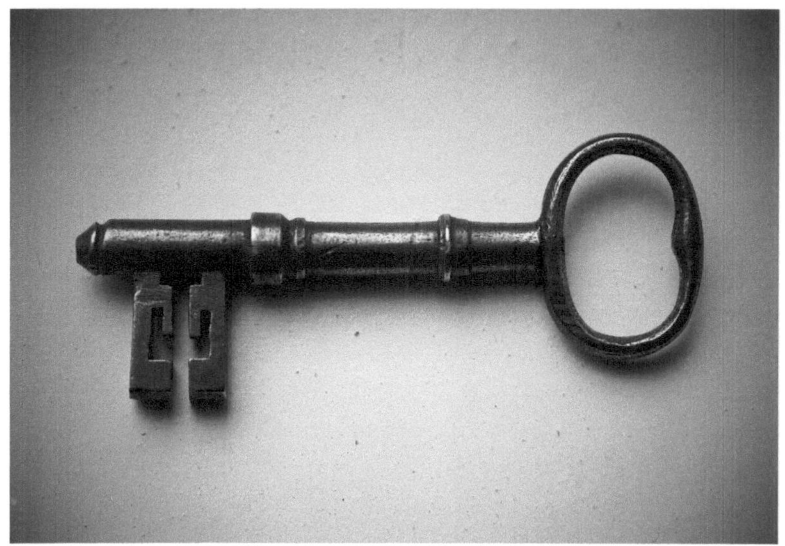

used the match to study the license. Then I turned the wallet inside out and found a key in a hidden slot. I looked at the woman's picture again.

I walked four blocks to the address on the driver's license. Nice neighborhood, nice building, well lighted, with good-looking cars parked out front. I found the name on the mailbox in the lobby, then went up the stairs. A square of gray cardboard was thumb-tacked beneath the door number.

It said: "Be right back. Went for cigarettes. Love Rose."

Both the O in love and the O in rose were little heart shapes.

I fit the key in the lock and let myself in.

The place reminded me of my mom's, except with better furniture. After she got cancer Mom suddenly qualified for an elderly housing program with reduced rent. She moved out of that shit hole she had raised me in and into a clean three-room apartment where she died a few months later.

I snapped lights on as I made my way to the kitchen.

The sink and counters were immaculate. The pine cupboards shined. There was a bowl of fruit on a square dinette table. I found some bread and put two slices on a plate. But there was no meat in the fridge. So I hunted through the cupboards until I found a jar of peanut butter, then used a chef's knife to make a sliced banana and peanut butter sandwich. I finished the sandwich in six bites and sat, playing with the knife, dropping it between my legs, watching the handle vibrate each time the tip stuck into the hardwood floor.

I was still hungry, wondering what else I might like to eat, when I heard the door, then a woman's voice: "Don? Honey?"

I waited, with my back against the wall.

You can tell a lot about people by the food they buy. In my kitchen, for instance, which I share with five other roomers, all degenerates, you'd find nothing that belonged to me. ■

Seaside Hitchhiker

THE MOON WAS BIG AND FULL AND UNUSUALLY BRIGHT. Its curious glow had followed me like a searchlight across thirty miles of interstate. On the curling beach road I slowed as I took the bend. I tried to find the moon reflected in the ocean. A girl swept across my high beams, her thumb high. I merely tapped the brakes, but the road was sandy and the rear of the car hooked. I skidded to a full stop like some high school punk showing off for his prom date.

She opened the passenger door and leaned in. A white long-sleeve shirt, soaking wet, clung to her swimsuit like lace. The car's dome light reflected in her eyes. She was somewhere between fifteen and twenty.

"Thanks for stopping, mister."

I told her I wasn't going far, just up the road a bit.

She gave a polite grin, shrugged. "Every little bit helps," and slid onto the seat.

Her hair hung like tangled seaweed and she stunk of the ocean, but she was attractive enough.

Once we got going, she twisted the rear-view mirror and lined her lips with a tube of pink lipstick. I kept one eye on the road, which ran parallel with the shoreline.

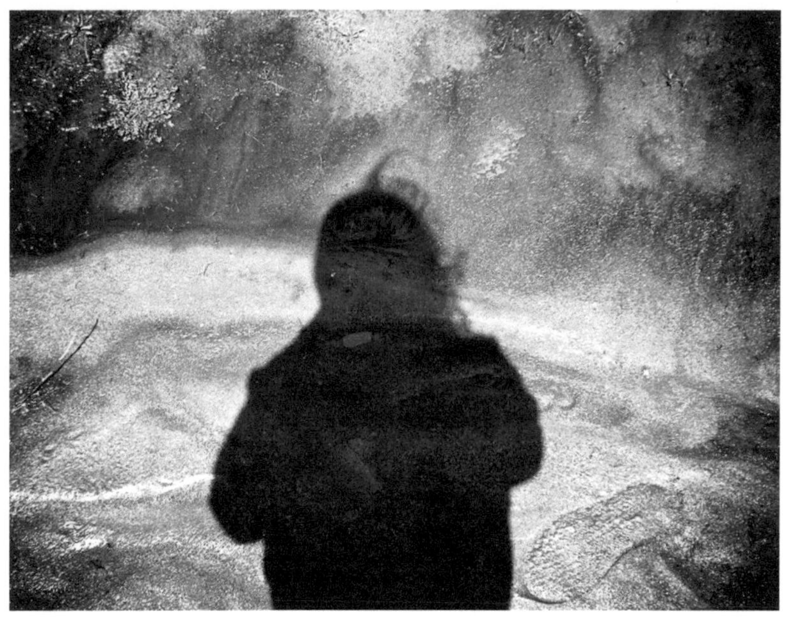

“There’s a mirror above the visor,” I said.

She puckered and dabbed. “This one’s fine.”

After she finished with the lipstick she tucked it into her shirt pocket. It bulged there, like a bullet. I readjusted the mirror. She caught me looking, moved her tongue across her teeth.

“You always swim at night,” I said.

“Not always.”

“You live around here.”

“Close enough.”

“Year round, or just for the summer?”

She pushed a hand through her hair. “I shouldn’t be telling you this, but I’m actually a mermaid, so I kind of live everywhere around here.”

“A mermaid, huh?”

“That’s right.”

My turn was just up ahead. "Where'd you get the lipstick? At the mermaid mall?"

"Found it. In the sand."

I tilted my head to see her legs. "Where are your fins?"

"Don't be silly. That's just myth."

I laughed, a little choking cough. She was either crazy or stoned. I held the wheel steady and sped past my turn. Our cottage, a summer rental my wife had found, was visible from this distance, but I didn't look to see if lights were on.

"Your parents know you're out this late?"

"It's not late."

"It's after midnight."

She shrugged. "My parents are dead. Sharks ate them."

"Sharks, huh?"

She shuddered. "Sharks gobble up mermaids the way you people eat potato chips."

I thought about letting her off, turning back. My wife was on vacation, but I wasn't. I had another long commute in the morning. "How do you know what people eat?"

"Oh, I come ashore a lot. I'm not afraid of people, just sharks."

"Where do you sleep?"

"Depends."

"You sleep on the beach?"

"Sometimes. Not often. I hate the smell of rotting seaweed. I much prefer a bed."

"A little sea bed?"

"Ha. That's funny." She brought her knee up onto the seat. "You have any money?"

"Why," I said.

She waited a while before answering. "There are motels up on the main strip. About five miles."

I knew about those motels. Ramshackle places. My wife had looked into their weekly rates, calculated the cost against the beach house.

"You hungry?" I said.

She shook her head.

"I'm hungry," I said.

She stuck her face out her window. The back of her blouse puffed and fluttered.

"So what do you do for money? How do you pay for food, motels?"

She twisted into a kneeling position, got her entire head and shoulders outside the car. Her swimsuit cut high on her thighs.

"Oh, I never pay," she said.

The Brine Motel was a line of small cabins beside an empty swimming pool. I paid in cash and took the key. The room was a box, rustic, smelled of disinfectant.

I asked if she preferred the light on or off and she laughed. "Makes no difference to me."

I like to see what I'm doing, so I left the bathroom's light on. Its glow spread a halo into the room. She undressed beneath the covers, peeling off one wet thing after another. I piled my clothes on a chair. She threw back the blanket, smiled as I climbed onto her.

"What's your name," I said.

"You'd never be able to pronounce it."

She kissed me on the mouth, then wiggled her hips, working her body down to get me centered. She held my ass with one hand and guided my penis with the other.

"At least tell me how old you are."

She shushed me and kissed my neck. "Honey, relax. By human standards, I'm a hundred years past legal."

She was slippery and tight, and she knew how to work her groin muscles. I didn't last five minutes.

"Jesus," I said, pulling breath. I hadn't gotten my wind when she nudged me off her. I rolled and flopped. I looked at the ceiling, then closed my eyes. Lying there felt familiar, and I decided this was my wife's fault. Somehow she was to blame.

I started to drift, then jerked awake, certain the girl had swiped my wallet, taken my car.

But she was right there, huddled forward on the edge of the bed. I could only see half her face, but she appeared older now, with hard creases along the side of her mouth.

She stretched her arms into a yawn. "I hate to be a prude, but I need to get some sleep." She threw her head back in an exaggerated fashion.

"I'm still hungry," I said, and reached for her.

I pulled her down and tried to pin her but she twisted free. She scrambled to her feet, backed away.

"Hey, look. You're a nice guy and all, but paying for a room doesn't make me your property. I think you better leave now."

But then I showed her my shark teeth. ■

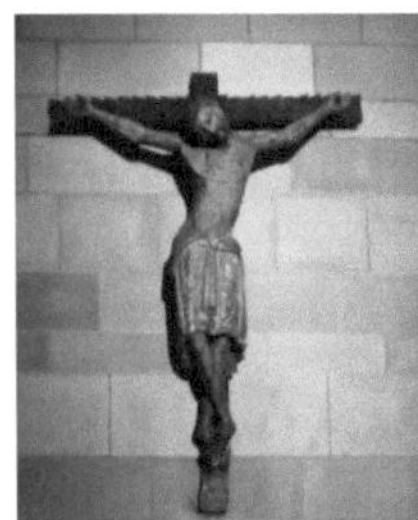
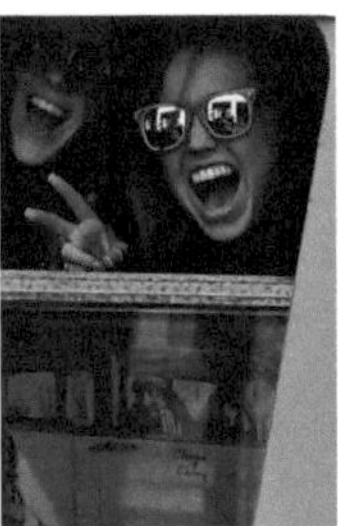
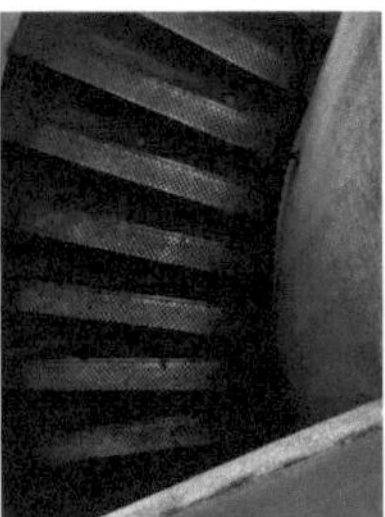
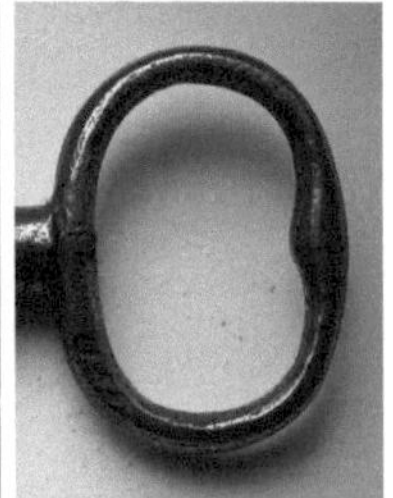

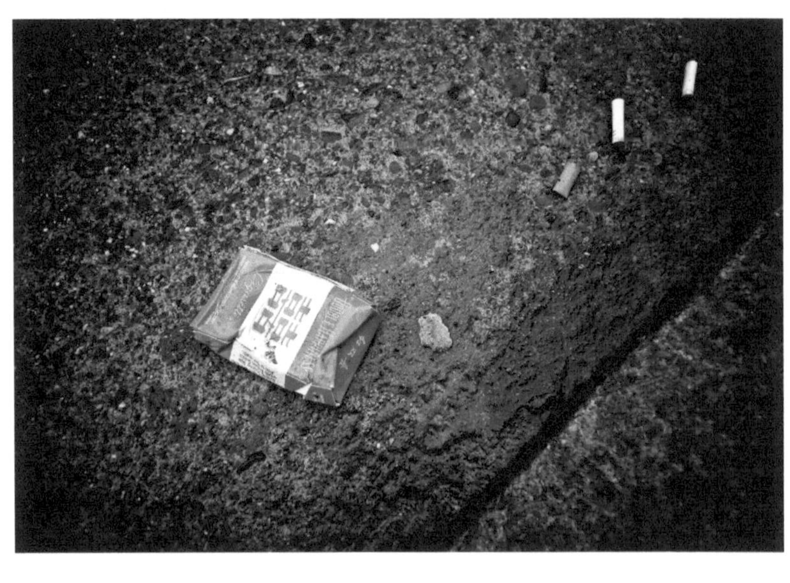

So Forth and So On

The Cat Who Waved

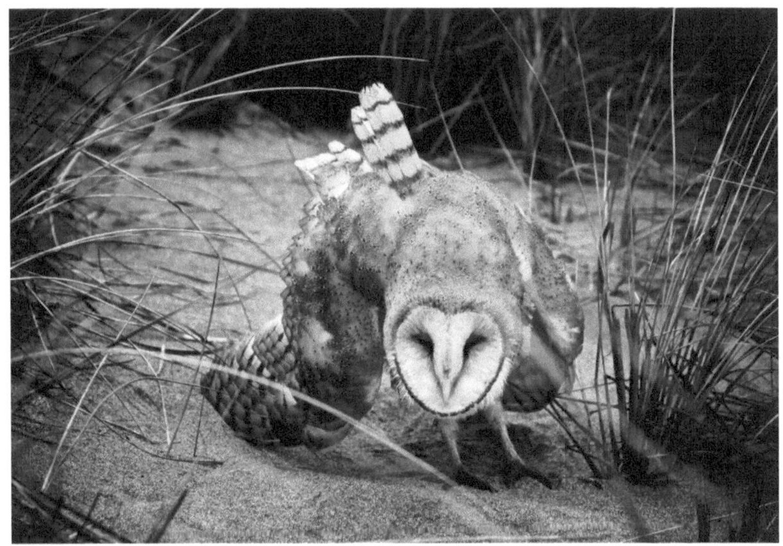

YOU WAKE IN BLUE DARKNESS AND THERE ARE TWO—TWO black-cat shapes curved against the glass, two sets of shining cat eyes. You count them to make sure. In poor light you're prone to seeing double, and you've had this dream before. This time you must be certain.

So you squint and focus and hold your breath. The thermal glass is two layers thick and tinted. You've seen its illusions before. Plus you've had alcohol, more than enough. And for a moment it is almost enough that, despite the glare of cat eyes, despite the perfect cat shapes, these could almost be pigeons, mere pigeons, just pigeons, because you are after all nine stories up, with a full moon painting shadows across your panoramic view.

It takes you nearly a minute to know for certain that they are cats, two cats on a ledge nine stories up, and how can that be? Whose cats?

Hoping to clear your head, you look away. You close your eyes for a three count, and then focus on the woman curled beneath the covers. You read the numbers on her clock, glowing like hot coals: 4:42. If you wake her, what could she say? Cats are climbers, dear, but nine floors, really? So you squint in the darkness, wondering if perhaps, just perhaps, they could be owls.

Owls, you've read, prefer to hunt from high places. They wait and watch for hours, then swoop down, talons splayed. They snatch their dinner on the fly and carry it back. They swallow their prey whole. Alive or dead, they don't care. Hours later, they cough up the gooey sacks of feathers, bones, fur.

You slide out of bed, tiptoeing like a thief. You require a much closer look. Your eyes aren't what they used to be. You tap the glass, trying to get them to turn, these two dark shapes. Owls can turn their heads 180 degrees. They have to. Their eyes are so large they have no room left for eye muscles. Barely room for brains.

For a brief instant four almond-shaped gems reflect moonlight. Then one cat turns away. The other, the smaller cat, stretches and drags a lazy paw against its side of the window, as if waving hello. You bang the glass with your knuckles, whispering, "Shoo, shoo!"

When the larger cat, without looking back, leaps, moving so fast, so catlike, that you don't see it go, you feel the air rush out of you. One moment there are two cats, now, only one. Your breathing stalls, stops, then starts as the cat who waved turns its head, looking for the other, bending its neck to peer over the ledge. Then it stretches again, spreading out, front paws extended, arching its back. It looks at you and yawns a great cat yawn. You press a hand to the glass. Then both hands. Then your face. The cold glass stings your forehead. You make a sound, not very loud, but loud enough that the woman stirs, wakes, sits up. But she is too late to see the second cat drop from the ledge.

"What is it?" she asks. "What's wrong?"

You step away from the window, studying your handprints in the fogged spot your breath has made. You tell the woman, "Go back to sleep. It was just two owls," believing that's what you saw, what you must have seen.

As you move toward the bed, straining to see her tousled hair and droopy bedroom eyes, you add: "But they flew off. They're gone now."

"Owls?" She yawns. "You were dreaming, honey. Come back to bed. There's not an owl within fifty miles of here." And she yawns again, moves her pillow, and she lowers her head. And you give her a minute to settle into sleep.

When she props herself up to turn on the light you've already got your pants on, searching on one knee for your other sock.

"Now what's wrong?" she says. "It's five A.M. Where on earth are you going?"

"Home," you say as you stretch your arm, straining the muscles, wiggling your fingers at something just out of reach. ■

Tarzan's Dream

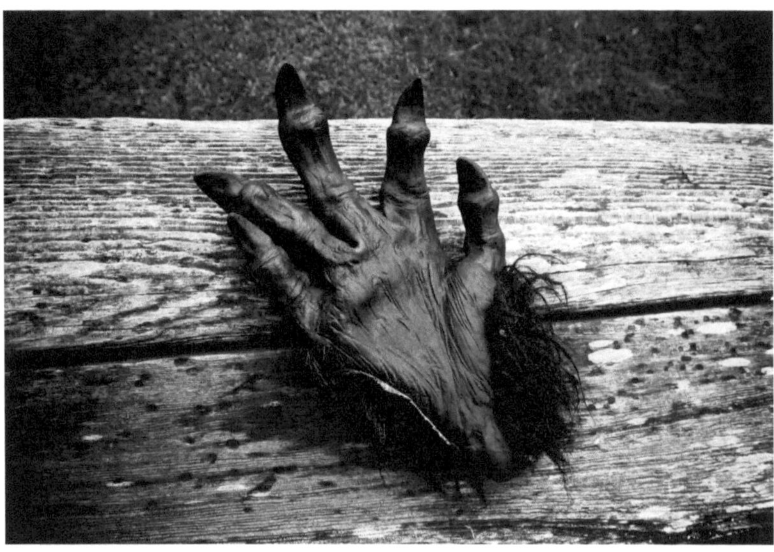

IN SCORCHING CITY HEAT BOY CAN'T SLEEP SO BOY WATCH movie—old, grainy, black and white adventure film. He watch on wall-sized plasma TV Jane buy Tarzan for wedding anniversary, then later take back to give Boy to watch in rented one-room studio, rent paid with alimony and child support sucked each month from Tarzan's bank account.

Boy have no taste in movies. Film on giant TV is crap. Monkey could do better. The interior monologue voice-over (performed by respected African American actor who played supervillain in Star Wars) so draining, within minutes Boy bored with plot, having no interest in hero (played by former Olympic Gold Medal Winner) who slightly resembles Boy's father. Film's story line simply that hero dream always about sleep, but cannot close eyes without room swirling, ceiling spiraling in cheap CGI effect stolen from Hitchcock.

Movie is a disgrace, two thumbs down, straight to video production. Hero is a schmuck, a clown, a chimp—overly concerned with personal development and self actualization, with natural increase in serotonin levels, and effortless redirection of superior brain cells, all of which hero believes will make him a better man. Hero so focused on all this drivel that his body refuse all food, all substance. He loses thirty pounds in eighteen day montage of flipping calendar. Hero's arms and legs become so puny he could not swim across a calm shallow river never mind fight a healthy crocodile. Yet in dream sequence hero is growing at such a phenomenal rate that the covers (i.e. two woolen blankets and one hand-stitched quilt and one cool satin over sheet that his American wife has been so thoughtful in supplying) appear no bigger than swatches from a fancy tailor's book, and our hero is freezing, lost in his shivering nightmare of sleeplessness.

Boy yawn and blink as on-screen hero twitches and jerks, both trying to readjust themselves because Boy is tired of being Tarzan's son, and hero is tired of playing movie idol, each weary of dreaming a frequent false dream in which the covers no bigger than swatches continue to shrink until they become as microscopic in size as the neurotransmitters Boy and hero have put all their faith in.

Boy find it embarrassing watching the hero lying bone naked in sleeplessness, and he becomes convinced ending will make him cry. The actor is such a sad case, no champion, just an antihero trapped in a cinematic hell, unaware that the best director in the modern movie-making world, utilizing state-of-the-art visual effects, is already fed up, millions over budget, and weeks behind his shooting schedule. Despite numerous previous successes director is doomed with this dog of a movie, this frequent false dream where our hero lingers on the brink of physical collapse, every brain cell shivering beneath a microswatch of comfort.

Boy thrilled when director screams Cut! Cut! and camera pulls back to show the camera pulling back, revealing a whole crew of movie-making professionals, eyes glazed over, jaws drooping, Boy's father among them, everyone unnerved by the unfit conclusion of this doomed dog of a movie (work is hard to come by when you've just come off a dog). The director storms toward his dressing room, waving his hand like a cavalry leader, indicating all should follow. But each crew member remains frozen, frowning at the hero, that pathetic soon-to-be out-of-work actor imitating sleeplessness by grinding his hips like Boy against the soft lumpy mattress in a rented one-room flat his big shot mother pays for.

The best-selling book on which this movie is based reveals the sordid ending to our hero's dilemma. Jane buy book for Boy but Boy doesn't read it. Full of angst, with no patience, no interest. Yet at moments like these each crew member refers to that section of their worn paperback copy (pages dog-eared or yellow-highlighted). They seek comfort in the eventual conclusion, holding to the hope that perhaps as soon as tomorrow the director will reschedule the filming of this final scene, the last ghastly chapter where the hero sits up, notices the world isn't watching, and sneaks back to the jungle, putting the brakes on Boy dreaming dreams he can never have, not in this city, not in this life, Boy being who he is, son of the mighty Tarzan. ■

Six Crows

All summer six bullying crows chased owls from my yard. Six of the biggest, blue-blackest crows I'd ever seen kept constant watch over my half acre of woods. I think it was six, the same six, just six, but one can hardly be sure when counting crows.

One morning I witnessed all six working together. I couldn't see where any owl had camped for the night. Six cawing crows soon pointed him out. The poor devil was perched in the low branches of the younger trees. I watched six crows dive bombing, swooping six at one time. They took turns; each gave a stunning solo performance.

After that first owl fled the crows returned in patrols of two or three. I used

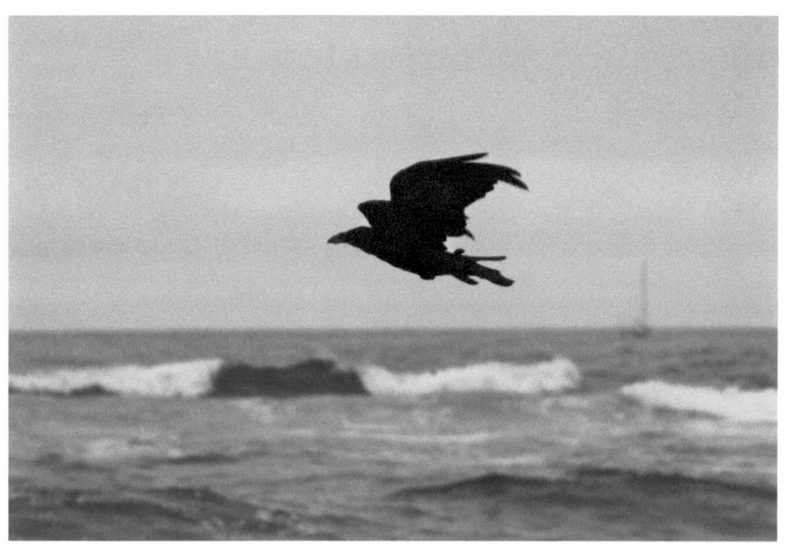

my father's field glasses to spy on each new owl. I studied markings. Never the same owl twice.

On Sunday my wife stopped by to visit. She still had her keys. She came in and set a chair beside my wheelchair.

I couldn't look at her.

She held my face in her hands but I averted my eyes.

Look at me, she said.

I could hear the crows cawing.

The strain hurt my neck. ■

A Note to Hansel, Thirty Years Later

Dear brother,

Forgive my delay in writing to you. I realize it's been thirty years. I hope you are healthy and happy and have remained so since our last meeting. For what it's

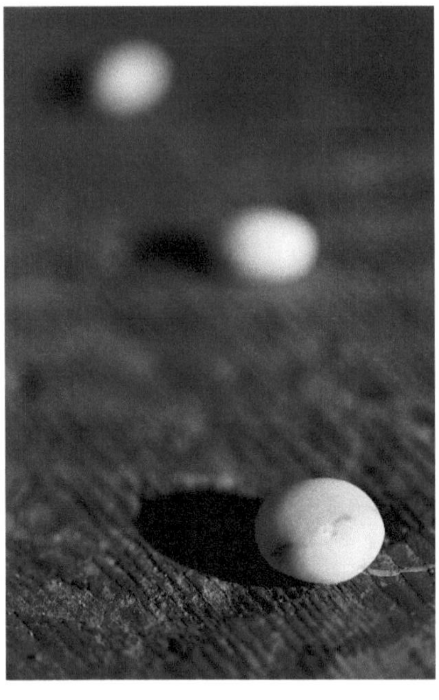

worth, I did send you an invitation to my wedding a couple of decades ago, though perhaps you had already moved by then and did not receive it. On the chance my hastily scribbled last minute invitation did find you, and you simply chose to ignore it, I understand. Water under the bridge, as they say. No hard feelings. No regrets. None directed towards you, at least.

Just last week I ran into someone from your neck of the woods, someone who knows you and our history, apparently. The whole story, more or less. Though she didn't go into specific detail, thank god. Or give me any slanted looks. Or ask for my autograph, which a surprising amount of people, especially children, still do. Anyway, this woman, who had fine clothes and an impressive feathered hat, says you've lost a surprising amount of weight. An amazing amount, she said. All your 'witch's fat,' she called it, this person who was half my age. Then she sighed and said you'd turned all your blubber into hard muscle, that you are no less handsome (she may have said 'hunky') as ever, with barely any lines (which she called 'distinguished') on your sun-bronzed face, and neat white hair instead of wild black (no doubt thick as ever.) I didn't remember the lady from any place, but she seemed to know you pretty well, said you had recently been hired to clear six acres of woodland for her husband. She seemed quite impressed by your work, so perhaps her husband can give you a letter of recommendation. Couldn't hurt. Though, and I mention this only because it struck me as odd, she made no mention whatsoever of the scar on your hand or whether you still wear a glove to conceal it when you work.

I'll get right to the point, my brother. I'm finally willing to admit you had the right idea. Okay? So that's done. That thorny issue is finally settled. You know how it is. Time permits reflection. Age brings clarity, if not wisdom. No question your mind was sharper than mine back then. Scattering crumbs to mark our trail, leaving a chance for return. Wonderful idea. Clever, resourceful. Though not at all practical, which was always my point. A smarter plan would have been to collect white stones from the lakeshore and drop one every few paces. Do you remember those stones, small as sparrow eggs and just as smooth, how we thought they had value, or held some power. You named them 'lake jewels' because wet or dry they shined, even in moonlight. You could have used those shining stones to dot a trail. A pocketful of lake jewels would have changed both our lives.

Believe it or not I still have a jar full that you gave me one year on my birthday, so many birthdays ago. I can't look at them, can't hold one in my hand without becoming annoyed. I remember being so angry that fateful day, and so tired, and so goddamn hungry. It hurt my head to walk. I couldn't think. I didn't realize father was leading us deeper into the forest than he ever had before. I was cramped, frustrated, ravenous. I hadn't had my period in weeks. Naturally I balked at the sight of you wasting our chunk of bread.

But you suspected what he was up to. You knew, and you played it cool.

Incidentally, how is it people still speak of a stepmother, a supposedly wicked femme fatale who manipulated father into abandoning us? How does such a rumor still linger when everyone within fifty miles knows the fool never remarried. Because what woman in those days or even now wants a deaf and dumb, ugly, drunken, worthless man?

But before I digress into my personal matrimonial woes, let me get back to the morning father carried his axe on his shoulder and we obediently followed behind, but not too close lest that silent, uncaring monster simply turn and murder us where we stood. Imagine if he had turned while I bitched and screamed, slapped and kicked. God forgive me, but I was ready to kill you over that chunk of bread. And when you held me off, almost effortlessly, I sunk my teeth into your hand and drew blood. I never told you this but I swallowed that small piece of flesh I tore from you.

Do you forgive me that scar, my brother? Do you forgive my absence all these years?

You have to understand, I felt like an animal, probably because we had always been treated like beasts, not children. And I was fed up. I had had it. And there you were tossing bread carelessly into the dirt. My bread. My supper.

But by the time we reached deep woods, though darkness had set in, you had calmed me down and wrapped your wound and convinced me of two things: one, a few bites of stale bread would have been a measly meal, deeply unsatisfying; and two, no one was suggesting we ever go back.

"It's just," you said, "that in life options are everything. They are everything, Gretel. Because they are all we have." Do you remember saying those words?

Even as a child you were so much smarter, seeing the world so much clearer than me.

Of course, by then we could no longer see the gleam of father's axe, or hear his feet rustling leaves, and we understood we had been abandoned, and then we discovered your trail of bread crumbs had vanished, and we knew we were lost.

I remember screaming until my throat hurt, panicked by the sounds of night creatures echoing all around and the cold gloom closing in, only the moon to warm us. I remember you making a bed of leaves, then holding me tighter than you ever had before, and I remember believing every word you told me, every whispered hope, and the warmth of your blood in my mouth as I sucked the wound I'd made in you.

So you quickly made a wound in me, tore me open with my legs on your shoulders. And when you were finished, I stood up knowing nothing except that I was changed, different, bloody, and confused.

What would our lives have become, I wonder, if at dawn we hadn't turned south, crossed the bridge, found that house built of confection and the half-blind hag who locked you in a cage, then forced me to clean and cook, feed you piles of fruits and cakes, one roasted creature after another. So much food for you and barely a crumb for me.

And how grotesque you became right before my eyes, slobbering away.

Do you remember the very last thing I fed you? A huge baked goose. A forty-pounder. I remember because I singed my hands tearing its flesh into chunks small enough to fit through the bars, just so I could lick the fat and juices off my fingers, all the while glaring at your blubbery face sunk deep in your massively swollen neck. How I hated your appetite and what you'd become. Not my brother, but a beast ready for slaughter.

And when that goose was devoured, instead of picking up the bones, I eyed the old hag leaning precariously into her oven, so I ran, threw all my weight into her, and shoved her bent broken body into the flames.

Do you know I still hear her screams whenever winter winds blow, that I still smell the stink of her burning flesh after every summer rain. It's in my head, I know, and I take a potion for that, but I still fall into fits of weeping, understanding it was the worst thing I ever did, shoving that hag into the fire, and the absolute right thing to do, the only choice I had to save you, that daring desperate act.

And I am not sorry for any of it. Though I often wonder how you cope with that memory. Please write and tell me where do you keep all the memories we made, all our special secrets.

I miss you, Hansel. I miss your smile, your eyes, your smell, your voice. I miss how you would carry me piggyback or over your shoulder or cradled high in your arms. I miss the lake jewels on our long walks and the short sprints we made to those crooks and caves and clearings that only you knew about. And how dizzy I would feel when we left them.

You never write, never visit. Not a word or a whisper in thirty years. Family should stay in touch. I blame the birds. Who do you blame? ■

Calling Home from a Phone Booth Outside a Pub in North Dublin

DESPITE AN ICY NORTHEAST WIND HUFFING ACROSS THE BAY, I sneak out after dark, after my mother falls asleep clutching her leather Bible, and I hike up the rutted road to the frosted meadow to stand in mist, my shoes in muck, and toss my echo against the moss-covered fieldstone corners of the

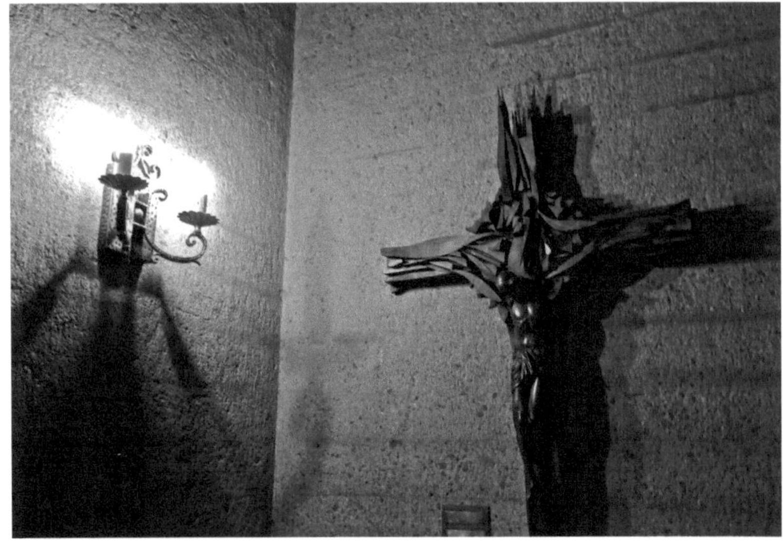

burned-out church where Sunday nights in summer for years Father Thomas, that mad handsome priest, would gather us girls in the basement to dye the rose cotton linen cut-outs that the deacon's daughter, a thin beauty with short white hair and long trim nails, would stitch by hand, each folded edge, then steam-iron flat, so full of starch, stiffening fabric petals, which we silly Sunday school girls curled with quick sharp pulls of a scissor blade, forming clusters of curved petals the younger children assembled with Krazy glue and fuzzy green wire, sometimes adding tissue paper leaves, all of us gladly laboring like factory workers rather than have to color with crayon stubs the robe of Christ again, Christ with his empty hands inviting us to dine, Christ with a shepherd's staff signaling to another flock of puffy lambs, or naked Christ with a drooping head crowned with blackened thorns, and Lord how we laughed later when we went door to door in groups, visiting the old parishioners, the sick and bittersweet, all the near dead, and we dropped our bikes on the perfect lawns of dull neighbors, agnostics we suspected, hawking our handmade linen roses for a donation, bragging how each petal was hand-cut from a pattern drawn by Father Thomas himself, that mad handsome priest, who personally told the Monsignor to go fornicate himself, saying he was a disgruntled altar boy calling home from a phone booth outside a pub in North Dublin, while I sat half-dressed, sniffing incense, giddy and drunk with sacrament wine stains on my panties, whispering my oath of unholy love while wiggling uncomfortably on the mad priest's lap, but God he was beautiful with a fine chiseled chin and perfect teeth and a smile that would melt the Madonna, and God he was kind with a slow gentle touch, never harsh or too quick, and Christ how that crafty devil could draw, imitate a rose petal in perfect outline, his sharp pencil slanted just so, the tip barely touching so that he could sketch and drink and cough without jerking, without ruining the work, or tearing the tissue paper, thin as a membrane, which like a clean skin arrived fresh each Saturday delivered by the dry cleaners, tucked into the crisp black vestment, wrapped around shirt cardboard, pinned to protect the high collar. ■

You Don't Belong Here

RECENTLY I RECEIVED AN INVITATION TO A SURPRISE fiftieth birthday celebration for an old friend. I don't have many friends. I could chop off my thumbs and still count the number of true pals on one hand. So when the invitation arrived, I decided I would make a genuine effort to attend the celebration.

I'm neither shy or gruff but I really hate parties. Over the years I've blown off dozens, hundreds of get-togethers, offended scores of people. The upshot is I'm seldom invited to anything anymore. When I am, I usually consider and reconsider, mulling it over for days, trying to persuade myself to go, but ultimately I don't attend. I'm constantly fearful I might run into myself.

If I do end up attending this party, I'll arrive early, I'll remain watchful, alert. Then, I'll make some excuse and leave early. It's safer that way. My doppelganger tends to show up fashionably late.

The last time I ran into him was eight months ago at my aunt's wake; I bumped into him in the funeral parlor's restroom. He was rubbing his hands under the blow-dryer, wearing the same suit as I was, though his jacket seemed to fit better.

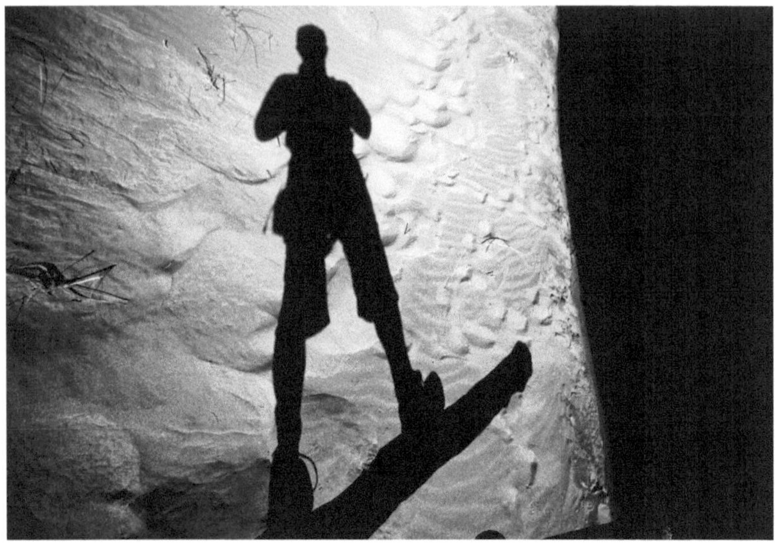

"Ah," we both said at the exact same time, "my evil twin."

After a long accessing stare, we both said, in the same tired voice, "You don't belong here. You should do yourself a favor and leave."

Another time, years before, at a wedding, I didn't actually see my doppelganger, though I'm certain he was there. I know because my wife disappeared for forty minutes while dinner was being served. The waitress kept asking, "Is anyone sitting here?"

I nodded each time.

I made excuses, gastronomical in nature, to the other guests at the table.

When my wife finally returned, her soup and entrée were sitting there, ice cold. Everyone else was waiting for desert.

A woman seated beside her said, "Feeling better now, hon?"

Another woman said, "You look a little flushed. Drink some wine, dear."

When I leaned and whispered, "Where the hell have you been?" she simply smiled.

No explanation. Just a dumb smile and a lingering gaze. Such an odd, tranquil look, as though we shared some secret.

On the ride home I asked again. "What were you doing all that time?"

She was silent, slumped low in the seat, eyes closed.

I decided she had fallen asleep so I focused on the road.

After a while she murmured, "You're a naughty boy for doing that."

"Doing what?" I said.

She was grinning again. "You might have at least allowed me time to put my diaphragm in."

I surmised the rest. I envisioned the scene and I felt myself heating up. I steered the car to the side of the road.

"What is it," she said. "Did we blow a tire?"

Too angry to look at her, I held my face in my hands. I said, "You mustn't confuse me with him. Not ever. You of all people should know better."

"Who and what are you talking about?" she said.

I was about to answer, ready to confess. I slowly removed my hands from my face. That's when I saw my car, or rather a car identical to my own, pull off the road and park a short distance ahead. I saw my doppelganger leap out and start toward us. He was waving one arm, dangling his keys. "You've gone too far this time," he shouted.

I glanced at the woman beside me. Her face was distraught. She couldn't have looked more confused, and I felt genuinely sorry for her.

"Who is that," she said.

I didn't answer. I sat there, nervously silent, understanding my mistake. I don't have many friends, but anyone who knows me understands I live alone, a solitary man who never married. You'd think I'd be able to remember that. ■

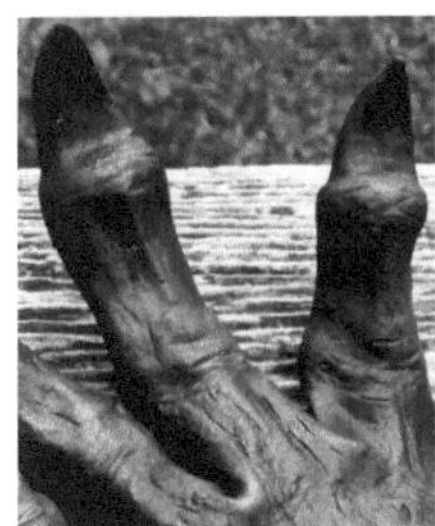
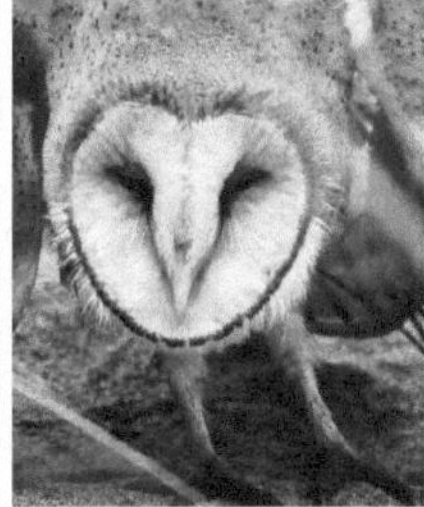
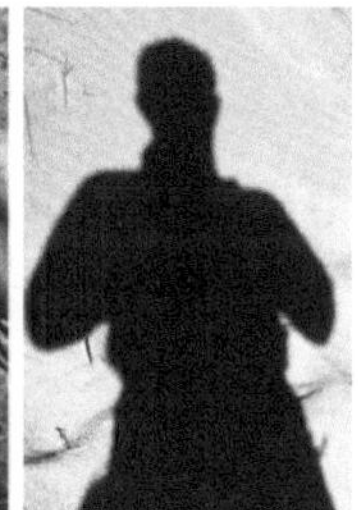
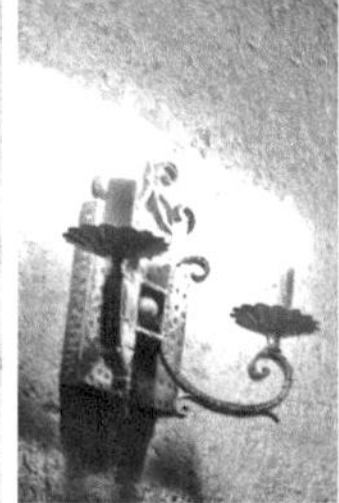

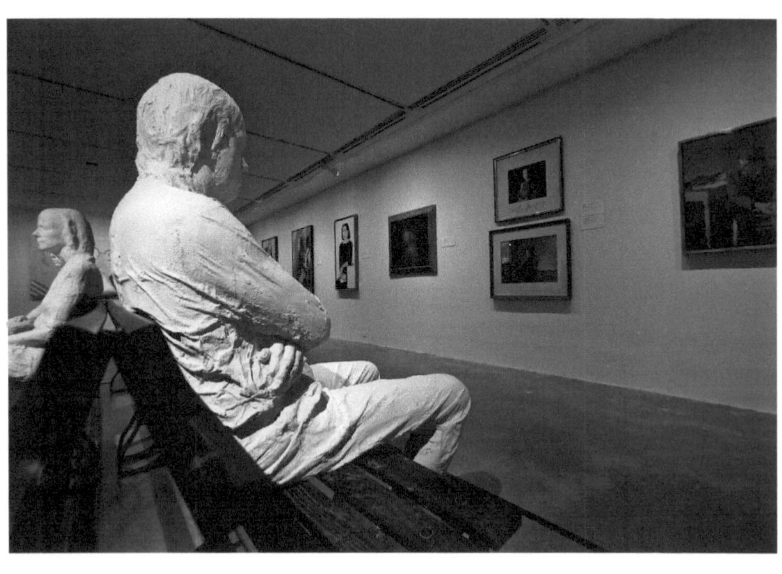

Art and Artifice

The Manuscript

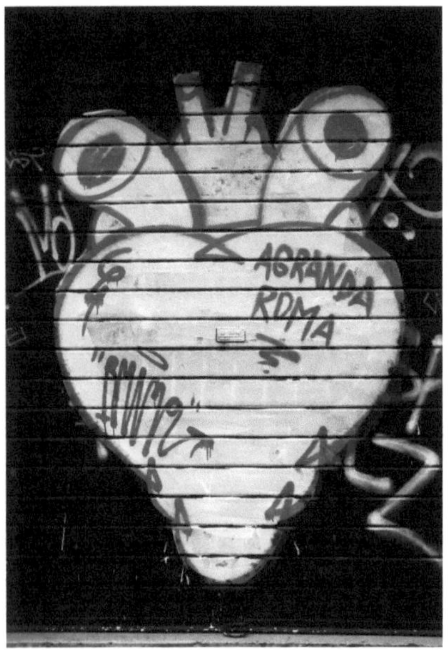

"When you write, you confront. You know this. We've covered this," the writer tells you. "Dynamic prose necessitates an encounter. Your reader advances from one direction, your text from another. Take this narrative," he says, curling the pages, "which I will concede is economically written. But something vital is missing. Do you follow?"

This is the part of the session you've come to hate.

"Can you name the missing component?" He is goading you, using your rolled up manuscript as a baton. "This story lacks . . . it lacks . . . ?"

But already your head is turned, pulled by the scent of perfume.

"Heart," the writer's wife says.

"Precisely," the writer says, looking up.

"No heart, no blood flow. I know about blood flow. Don't I, dear?"

She puffs a long cigarette in the archway that separates this tiny space from the rest of the house. Her nails are long sleek curves. You guess her age at forty something, slightly less than his.

"You don't look happy to see me, Roger." Smoke floats from her mouth. "Cat got your tongue?"

The writer, whose work you have read and barely understood, and who sometimes in lecture hall you stare at with the same watery gaze that he is now directing at his wife, that writer turns his eyes quickly to you, loops an arm around your shoulder, and gently steers you toward the exit.

"We'll talk more," he says in a near whisper.

There are never any working clocks in the writer's office, and today your watch needs a battery. Still, you're certain your time isn't up. The writer is giving you the bum's rush, and you don't blame him. You're hurting your neck, straining to see the pretty wife.

In the larger, friendlier room beyond the office, the room with the fireplace and the couch that shines like chocolate pudding, the writer's wife snaps on a light and strikes a pose.

She's wearing a man's pinstriped suit with a floppy bow in place of a necktie. The wide lapels make her look sharp, daring, like a gangster. Her fragrance has changed the air, somehow expanded this cramped off-campus cottage that you dread visiting twice a week. According to your mother you are allergic to both smoke and perfume, but today you are in no hurry to leave.

"Next week, then," says the writer, handing you your raincoat.

But you can tell by his wife's clothes and hair that it has stopped raining. You feel no need for the coat, have no desire to hold it.

"You've read my story?" you say to the wife.

She floats back into the doorway, trailing smoke, new light bouncing off her cheekbones. "Excuse me?"

You decide she is less than forty, much less.

"My story, you . . . " But that is all you can manage. Your jaw goes slack as you imagine her naked, standing exactly where she is standing now, smoking her long cigarette.

"She's joking," the writer says. "She doesn't read my students. Do you?"

You like her mouth, her eyes, the way she is looking at you. You believe you better understand the writer, that his arrogance is misunderstood.

If you were him you'd never leave the house.

"Roger hasn't taught me to read. Have you, Roger?"

You delight in her full windup as she tosses her cigarette into the dead fireplace.

The writer is showing you his yellow teeth. You can't remember ever seeing him smile this long, and for a moment you imagine him something less than a main character in his own life.

"You promised not to patronize me in front of my students, sweetheart."

"And you promised never to call me sweetheart, sweetheart."

She retreats toward a mirrored wall with a horseshoe-shaped bar and four padded stools. You admire her skill at balancing on such thin heels. You can barely see the mirror until you move slightly left, away from the writer. Then the mirror finds you, then there are two rooms, two of her.

"Excuse me," the writer says, and releases your manuscript to uncurl atop your raincoat. You trap it there, following the writer at a safe distance as he shuffles his penny loafers from floor onto carpet. For the first time today you notice his socks don't match.

"What are we doing?" the writer says.

His wife is grinning, looking at you more than at the writer.

Then she ducks from view as though the floor behind the bar just collapsed.

"You don't have to stay for this," the writer tells you, as his wife comes up swaying a goblet. She waves it at the room, at the writer, then at the you in the mirror. Her other arm moves like a snake.

"Lori, don't make a game of this," the writer says. "I have another student coming."

He leans awkwardly, both hands on the bar. His arms appear too thin to support his weight. You wait for him to collapse, while he waits for some response from his wife who is examining a bottle she brought up to the bar. Black, with a netted bottom, it reminds you of something your father might drink.

The writer is watching you, studying your face as you watch his wife twist the cork out with her teeth.

"Drink?" she says.

You don't belong here, your time is up.

The writer's face is saying this, not you.

"This is exactly the problem," the writer says. "Right here. Lori, listen to me. This young man is a student. He needs to be here. I am not obligated to entertain, but I am required to read and critique the good ones. As it happens, he's one of the good ones. Lori? Do you think this is fun for me? Do you think I care about some thousand page memoir a farm boy wrote. This is the job. This is what we signed on for. Lori! For god's sake at least tell me what you're doing?"

But any fool could have seen. ■

Oath

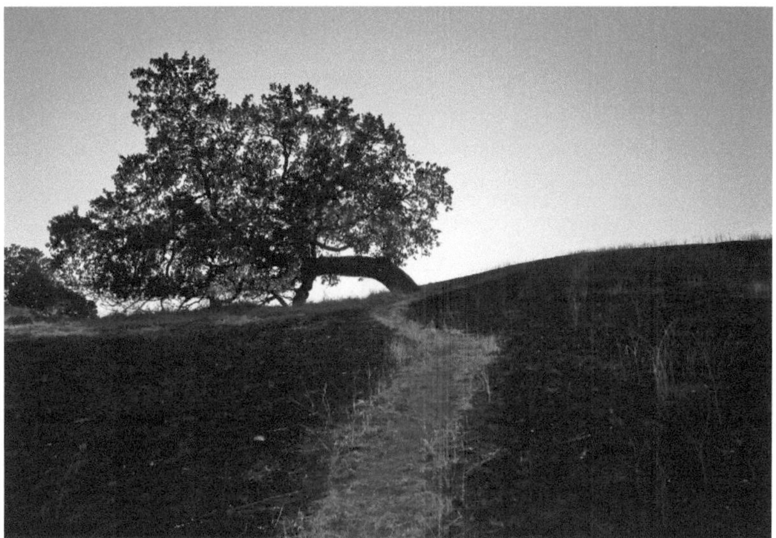

TRUE STORY. SO HELP ME GOD.

In Family Court, late 1991, I listened to my ex-wife swear to tell the truth, the whole truth and nothing but.

So help me god, she said.

Straight-faced and glassy-eyed she told a courtroom full of strangers what she'd been telling friends right along—what a worthless waste of human spirit I truly was.

Her attorney, who was better dressed than mine, asked: How often did the plaintiff visit his daughter after your divorce?

My ex didn't hesitate, didn't blink.

Maybe twice, she said.

I leaned into my lawyer.

She's lying. I said.

He raised his legal pad on which he had written nothing and used it to hide our mouths. Relax, he said. They do it all the time.

I had no documentation, no proof I'd visited every Tuesday, no evidence that each week I handed cash to my vindictive ex and listened to her bullshit just so I could see my daughter for a few hours. Toward the end, my new wife accompanied me on numerous visits, but her testimony wasn't allowed on the grounds of prejudice.

After a short recess the judge denied my request for joint custody and regular visitation. Then he terminated my parental rights on the grounds of abandonment and non-support.

So help me god.

Numb, woozy, I staggered to my feet. I couldn't remember how to leave the courtroom. My lawyer put his hand on my shoulder and guided me like he was escorting a blind man.

We need to talk before you leave the building, he said.

I located my new wife, front row center. Her eyes were moist, but she wasn't crying. I watched my daughter hop out of her seat and follow her mother out of the courtroom.

So help me god.

I said to myself: For the rest of your life, you will remember this moment.

My lawyer rode down with us in the elevator, just us three. He spoke about the appeal process. This is not over yet, he said. It's far from over.

My wife clutched my arm and squeezed.

Take a few days, then call my office, my lawyer said. Make an appointment to come in and we'll discuss your options.

He was noticeably thrown by the judge's ruling. And friendlier then ever.

Don't think this is over, he reminded us.

My wife shook his hand and that handshake turned into a hug.

Thank you so much for everything, she said.

I had thirty days to file my appeal, but why bother. No judge was going to take my word on anything. I was a writer with no regular income. My wife supported my existence, which officially made me a chump, a loser.

So help me god.

Time heals nothing. Wounds fester and ooze. Life drags you by a rope over rocks and stones and one day you look up, look back, and see you've been used to cut a path, mark a trail.

So help me god. ■

In the "Nick of Time" Redux

RECENTLY MY DAUGHTER SENT ME AN EMAIL IN RESPONSE TO an email I'd sent her a few days before. She lives on the west coast with her cats, and I live on the east coast with my dogs. We don't talk often, and when we do, we don't say much.

My email had contained a link to a photograph from a Twilight Zone episode titled "Nick of Time." That episode, from 1959, is about a honeymoon couple's experience with an unusually accurate fortune telling machine and starred a young William Shatner, who later went on to play starship Captain James T. Kirk on the original Star Trek series.

In the Twilight Zone episode, Shatner's character, Don Carter, and his pretty young wife find themselves temporarily stranded with a broken-down car in a small midwestern town. The newlyweds end up in a restaurant, in a booth, feeding pennies to a fortune telling machine, directing questions of fate and fortune to the bobbing, plastic head of a horned devil.

In the photograph that I sent to my daughter, Mr. and Mrs. Carter are posing with the sinister machine. William Shatner's mouth is open, as is the devil's. My message to my daughter read: Penny for your thoughts.

In her reply, she wrote: You have way too much time on your hands.

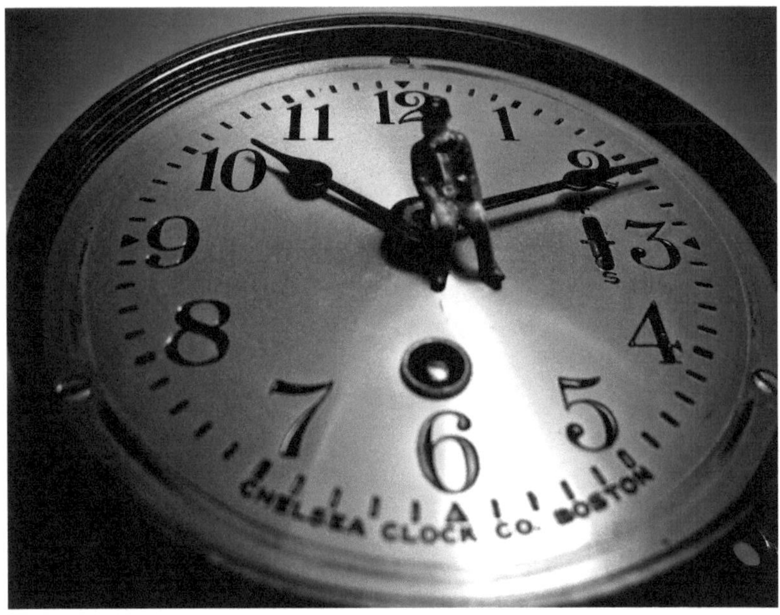

The message contained nothing else.

She's absolutely right, of course.

In middle age I discover time, though no longer on my side, is frequently on my hands.

Each day, as I set out to create narratives, to tell careful stories, subjective time flows from the tips of my long fingers. Creating narrative is a dreamy business but a tough job, harder than I thought it would be or should be when I explored the idea some thirty years ago, and now I find not only time on my hands, but blood. Deep pinkish stains. Most of it is my daughter's blood.

We don't talk very often.

Ironically, I received her reply on the tenth of April, which happens to be the date her mother and I were married.

That marriage did not work out well.

Shortly after my daughter's birth, that marriage imploded with a dull groaning extended popping noise, like the sound, I imagine, a ship makes when trapped in Antarctic ice, the pressure of the ice forcing the ship to rise out of the water (if it has been designed properly with a round bottom) or giving way to the force, the timbers cracking, snapping like dry twigs (if the hull's angle is steep, not designed for ice lock).

Twenty-six years later, I find parts of that marriage stranded on the ice. A cold memory. Still alive. Still living. Managing to find nourishment in seal flesh, using seal blubber to fuel a small stove, using seal skins to patch the tears the icy wind rips in the ancient tents. Twenty-six years on the ice.

Memory in the mind of man can adapt to the worst conditions.

I'll give you an example, an analogy of sorts: Each night I sop rags with beer and lay them out in careful strips. With rags soaked in beer I tease cockroaches from a crack in the baseboard. By morning they're good and drunk and I pop them into a baggy, then take them outside and throw the little buggers away.

"That's so gross," my daughter said.

She had called, long distance, to wish me a happy something or other. It was awkward. We don't talk often.

"Memories are worse than cockroaches," I said.

After a long silence, she said, "Why do you say such things, why do you act that way, why can't we ever have a normal father daughter conversation?"

For a moment I had no words. Imagine that. Me. A man who has spent his entire adult life arranging words.

So I said, "Too much time on my hands, I guess," then I hung up the phone just as I would on a stranger. ■

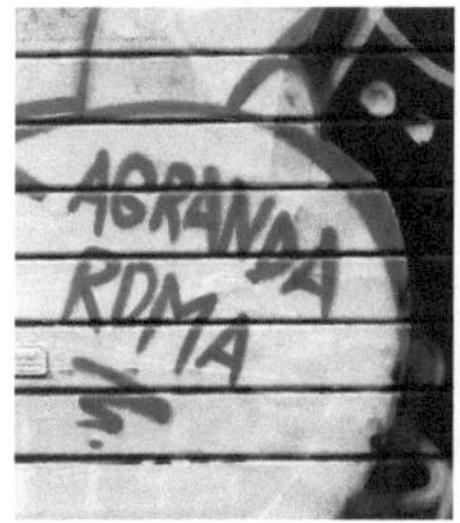
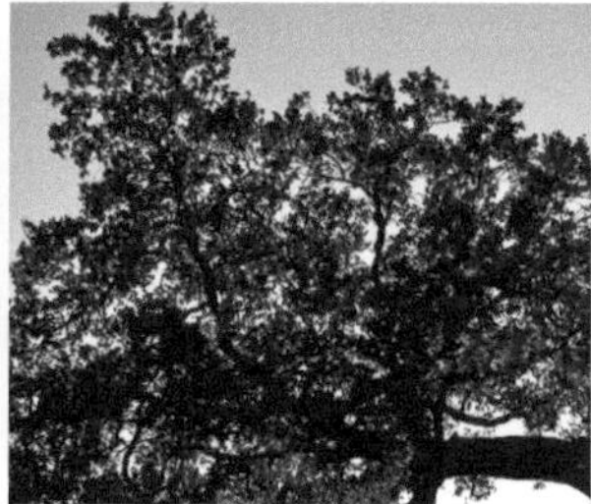
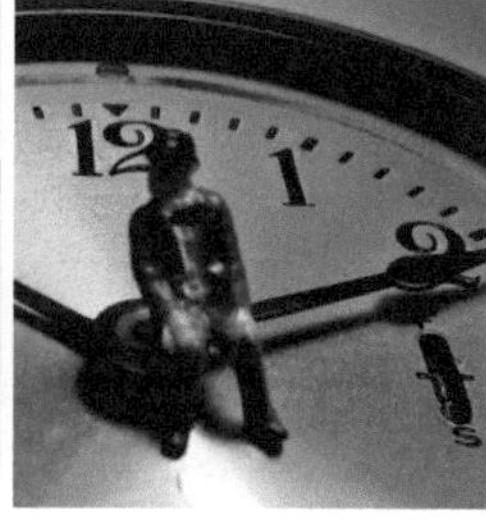

Bob Thurber - Biography

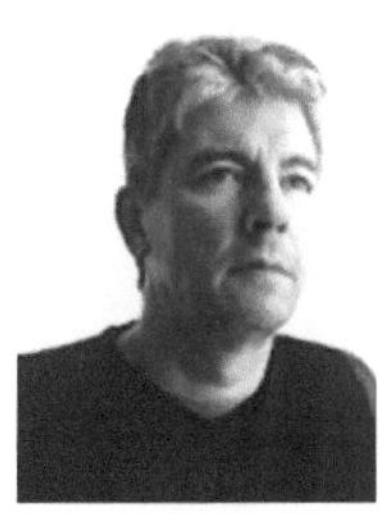

Bob Thurber (b. 1955) grew up "dirt poor" in Rhode Island where he graduated public high school "by the skin of his teeth." At the age of nineteen, he bought an electric typewriter and set out to become a writer. Thurber never took a writing class and has no academic credentials or degrees. Despite his lack of education, he studied and wrote every day for over twenty years and sold his first story at the age of forty-two. He has gone on to publish over two hundred more stories and has received over fifty literary awards and citations. His work has appeared in thirty anthologies. Thurber has been called *a raw and unique talent, a maestro of micro-fiction, an emotional terrorist,* and *The Sam Peckinpah of Flash Fiction*. His work is frequently used in schools and colleges as examples of concise prose. Thurber now lives in Massachusetts, where, despite vision loss, he still writes every day.

Thurber's debut novel, *Paperboy: A Dysfunctional Novel* (Casperian Books), was released in 2011 and received much critical acclaim. That was followed by *Nickel Fictions: 50 Exceedingly Brief Stories* and *Cinderella She Was Not: A Novelette* in 2013. ■

www.bobthurber.net

Vincent Louis Carrella - Biography

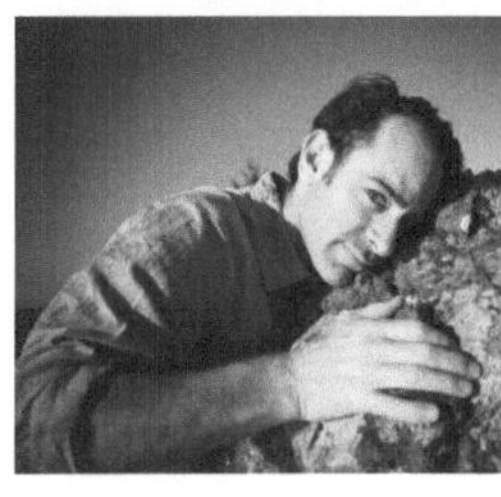

VINCENT LOUIS CARRELLA is a photographer and writer living in northern California. He writes "The Light Box Shaman," a column for *Stone Voices* magazine that explores the intersection of synchronicity, the subconscious, memory, and photography as a means of personal divination. His novel *Serpent Box* (Harper Perennial, 2008) follows the tragic life of a ten-year-old snake-handling boy living in rural Tennessee circa 1946. Carrella's blog (also called *Serpent Box*) is a photographic journal of self-discovery and odd coincidence. He has two daughters. ■

serpentbox.wordpress.com

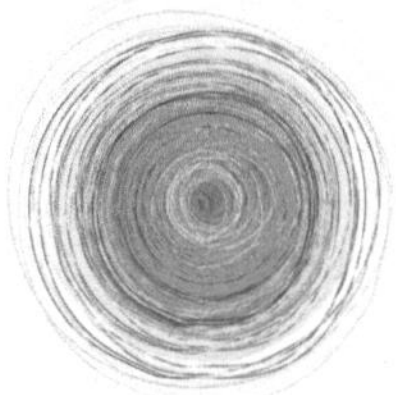

Art and artistry transform the world.

SHANTI ARTS celebrates and promotes art and artistry through exhibitions and publications. If you enjoyed this book and would like to find out about our other books, we invite you to visit us online. There you will find a complete list of our book and serial publications as well as information about exhibitions, artist and writer opportunities, and book submissions. Our books may be purchased on our website, through most online booksellers, and at many fine bookstores.

If you would like to receive mailings about our exhibitions and publications, please visit our website and add your name to our mailing list.

www.ingramcontent.com/pod-product-compliance
Lightning Source LLC
LaVergne TN
LVHW052304100826
845147LV00006B/672